Hell Is Dark with No Flowers

The Snake-Eating Inn

Yoru Michio

YEN ON
New York

Hell Is Dark with No Flowers 3
The Snake-Eating Inn

YORU MICHIO

Translation by Taylor Engel
Cover art by Maiko Aoji

JIGOKU KURAYAMI HANAMONAKI Vol.3 HEBI KURAU YADO
©Yoru Michio 2019
First published in Japan in 2019 by KADOKAWA CORPORATION, Tokyo
English translation rights arranged with KADOKAWA CORPORATION, Tokyo through
TUTTLE-MORI AGENCY, INC., Tokyo.

English translation © 2025 by Yen Press, LLC

Yen On
150 West 30th Street, 6th Floor
New York, NY 10001

Visit us at yenpress.com • facebook.com/yenpress • twitter.com/yenpress
yenpress.tumblr.com • instagram.com/yenpress

First Yen On Edition: May 2025
Edited by Yen On Editorial: Emma McClain
Designed by Yen Press Design: Lilliana Checo

Yen On is an imprint of Yen Press, LLC.
The Yen On name and logo are trademarks of Yen Press, LLC.

Library of Congress Cataloging-in-Publication Data
Names: Michio, Yoru, author. | Engel, Taylor, translator. | Aoji, Maiko, artist.
Title: Hell is dark with no flowers / Yoru Michio ; translation by Taylor Engel ;
cover art by Maiko Aoji.
Other titles: Jigoku kurayami hanamonaki. English
Description: New York : Yen On, 2024-
Identifiers: LCCN 2024021720 | ISBN 9781975379384 (v. 1 ; trade paperback) |
ISBN 9781975379407 (v. 2 ; trade paperback) | ISBN 9781975379421 (v. 3 ; trade paperback) |
ISBN 9781975379445 (v. 4 ; trade paperback) | ISBN 9781975379469 (v. 5 ; trade paperback) |
ISBN 9781975379483 (v. 6 ; trade paperback) | ISBN 9781975379506 (v. 7 ; trade paperback) |
ISBN 9798855409529 (v. 8 ; trade paperback)
Subjects: LCGFT: Horror fiction. | Monster fiction. | Light novels.
Classification: LCC PL873.I35 J5413 2024 | DDC 895.63/6—dc23/eng/20240523
LC record available at https://lccn.loc.gov/2024021720

ISBNs: 978-1-9753-7942-1 (paperback)
978-1-9753-7943-8 (ebook)

10 9 8 7 6 5 4 3 2 1

LSC-C

Printed in the United States of America

Contents

Mystery 1   Ushioni, or Nureonna   1

Mystery 2   Himamushi Nyuudou,
                or Sunekosuri   79

Mystery 3   Filicide, or Epilogue   155

Takamura Ono

A mysterious man dressed in Heian-period clothing. Always there before you notice him.

Seiji Tohno

Shiroshi's assistant. He can see other people's sins at a glance.

Major Characters

Illustrations by Maiko Aoji

Shiroshi Saijou

A beautiful, enigmatic boy who counsels troubled people.

Beniko

A mysterious girl with eyes like black glass.

Odoro Rindou

The famously sharp "Detective Who Summons Death."

Do they come when misfortune calls, or do they bring misfortune with them?

Ibara Rindou

Odoro's twin brother.

Mayuka Asaka

A hostess at the inn.
Has an eye like Seiji's.

Ranko Asaka

The inn's proprietress.
Kuniomi's second wife.

Kazutora Sawada

The inn's head clerk.

Kuniomi Asaka

Mayuka's father. Killed in
a random attack sixteen
years ago.

Suzu Torikai

A client of the Rindou
Detective Agency.

MYSTERY 1

USHIONI, OR NUREONNA

In this world, there may be an *oni*-eating snake.

*

It was dusk, the time of day when you had to ask, *Who goes there?*

Up ahead, the road ran on and on between black board fences. When Seiji looked back, an ominously intense light still lingered in the sky, as if burning down from its western edge. It was the color of flames, or maybe of fresh blood.

Either way, sunset came way too quickly, he grumbled to himself. He started walking faster, his worn-out sneakers dragging a bit.

Frankly, he'd underestimated the saying "In autumn, the sun sets like a bucket falling into a well." He'd left the house a little after noon, so he should have had plenty of time, and yet…

Right out of the gate, he'd made the rookie mistake of mixing up Kanda Station and Jinbocho Station, just because the first character in their names looked the same on paper. The information center staff had gotten disgusted with him after he came in to confess that he was lost for the third time, and then he'd fallen asleep on the subway home and slept way past his station.

People really shouldn't do stuff they're not used to, huh?

Trekking around used bookstores, for example.

Technically, Seiji should have had as little to do with the Kanda Used

Book District as polar bears did with tanning salons. To begin with, even books had the right to choose their readers.

If I'm remembering right, the word tasogare—*"twilight"—comes from* "Tasokare."

Tasokare was an old phrase meaning "Who goes there?" Even the more poetic term for twilight, the "hour of demons," referred to the time of day when it grew hard to make out the faces of people on the street.

Day and night, illusion and reality, human and inhuman: This time was a borderland where opposites mingled.

Right now, Seiji was hurrying home because of his left eye. When the hour of demons came around, he tended to run into yokai—or rather, criminals—on their way to the mansion where he was freeloading.

When he was five, a fragment of the Mirror of Illumination had fallen out of the sky and into that eye. Ever since then, people who'd committed sins had looked like yokai to him.

On top of that, the European-style mansion where Seiji lived had a spell on it that caused sinners to wander in at twilight—because its owner ran a proxy service for Hell.

Basically, that house was Hell's branch office. The client was Great King Enma himself, and the job involved finding sinners who'd escaped punishment for their crimes in this world and sending them to Hell.

Shiroshi was the "demon" lying in wait at the house. He'd bought— erm, *hired*—Seiji when he was on the run from loan sharks and living out of net cafés.

Seiji had been his live-in assistant and freeloader for ten months now.

Maybe it was true that your experience in Hell depended on the *oni* you were dealing with: Although Seiji had witnessed some unbearably ghastly things, somehow or other, the days had passed peacefully.

Or at least they had until that summer.

We still don't really know a thing about what happened back there.

The incident occurred three months ago, in August.

They'd responded to a suspicious letter of invitation and gotten dragged into a murder case on a remote island in Nagasaki Prefecture. As a result, they'd uncovered a conspiracy revolving around Shiroshi.

At first, it had appeared that the culprit was Hibana, Shiroshi's youngest elder brother, who'd died before Shiroshi was old enough to know him. Both he and the caster who'd resurrected him had lost their lives when the case was solved.

However…

Who was actually behind it?

In the end, they still knew nothing about the mastermind, the real culprit. They didn't have a single clue to their identity or their circumstances.

Tasokare—*who goes there?*

The old superstition was probably correct: The one that wouldn't answer the question "Who are you?" was the true *oni*.

"I'm back!"

When he finally got home, Seiji jogged through the front door—which was always standing open—then hustled up the L-shaped stairway that circled the entrance hall. He didn't really need to be sneaky, but he was a little embarrassed about the purchase he'd made that day, so he stopped by his room on the second floor before hurrying back down to the study.

Tea was usually around four in the afternoon. Seiji had assumed he was disastrously late, but…

"Huh? Wait, it's only four thirty?"

When he checked his smartphone and saw the time, he did a double take. Not having to make excuses was great, but even if early sunsets were one of the things autumn did best, this was ridiculous.

"…Hm?"

As he was hurrying down the hall to the study, Seiji stopped in his tracks. The occupant of the goldfish bowl in the bay window had caught his eye.

It was a high-class goldfish known as a *torachoubi*, with scarlet scales and a black, butterfly-shaped tail. As it swam, tail flowing elegantly, it looked just the way it always did. But on closer inspection—

"My, what's the matter?"

When Seiji turned, he found Shiroshi standing there.

Shiroshi Saijou was a beautiful boy with black hair and eyes. Although he appeared to be fifteen or sixteen, he was actually a half-human, half-yokai supernatural who ran this proxy service for Hell. In fact, he was the noble son and heir of Sanmoto Gorouzaemon, the Demon King who'd made a cameo appearance in the *Ino Mononoke Roku.*

A single white peony, its outlines ombré-dyed in black, bloomed on his white kimono.

The king of a thousand flowers.

"Um, there are little white bumps around its fin."

"Oh, yes, the pearl organs," Shiroshi answered easily. Seeing that Seiji still had questions, he went on. "Male goldfish develop those white spots near their pectoral fins during the spawning season. It usually happens in spring and autumn; he's a little late this year."

So the goldfish was male? Since it resembled Shiroshi's attendant Beniko, Seiji had just assumed it was female. Apparently, he'd been way off.

"Well, shall we repair to the study? I'm told there's a new offering on the menu today."

Glad tidings indeed!

Cheerfully getting his hopes up, Seiji followed Shiroshi through the door at the end of the hall.

A familiar sight greeted him: drapes that framed the windows like theater curtains; a bookshelf that covered the whole right-hand wall from floor to ceiling; and—

"Please be seated."

Beniko stood in front of the table, which was already laid for tea. As always, she was dressed like a Japanese maid in scarlet and black, the same colors as the goldfish.

"Well, I'm quite looking forward to this." Smiling, Shiroshi pulled out his usual Queen Anne chair. Seiji sat down in his own spot across the table from the boy.

"…Huh? It's apple pie, like always? I thought it was something new."

"It does appear to be apple pie, but I believe the filling is sweet potato."

Whoa. Talk about an autumn classic. The piping hot pastry was topped with a small white mound of cold whipped cream. When a sauce generously studded with cubed apples was poured over that—

"Th-this is gonna be amazing!"

"Heh-heh-heh. It's rather delicious just to look at, isn't it?"

The pair got far too excited for their ages, and Beniko's profile looked a little proud.

"There you are. Please enjoy."

They clapped their hands together once, as if in worship, then scrambled to pick up their forks.

The piecrust crunched in a light, tasty way as Seiji sank his teeth into it. The mere sound was delicious. Then the simple sweetness of warm sweet potatoes mingled with the cool, smooth cream and the tart, crisp apples.

"I'd like to cough this back up so I can eat it again."

"Heh-heh. If you were a cow, you could. Shall we have another piece?"

"Absolutely, yes!"

Beniko, who'd made a trip back to the kitchen, returned with the tea wagon.

Could it be?! As they watched in intense anticipation, she stopped the cart beside the table. She already had two plates of hot sweet potato pie on standby, complete with whipped cream and apple sauce. Seiji was pretty sure he could see a holy light emanating from those plates.

Okay, that settles it. He resolved not to regain his sanity until after he'd asked for thirds.

Once he'd split the last slice with Shiroshi and had polished off a total of three and a half pieces...

There was a brief, electronic noise, and Shiroshi got out a smartphone.

"Excuse me. I have a text."

Yes: Two weeks ago, he'd finally bought his own phone.

"Wow, that's you all over! You've already got flick input down?!"

"Yes. Still, these are a bit of a problem, aren't they? Once you've grown accustomed to them, it feels as if you may never be able to go without again."

"Yeah, they're really convenient. You can watch movies and TV shows on them these days, and you can even set up an Instagram account if you want."

"Heh-heh-heh. Selfies don't interest me, but I'm quite taken with the idea of pet photos."

…Okay, I'm pretending I didn't hear that.

Still, he seems more cheerful than I thought he was. That's good.

The incident in Nagasaki seemed to have taken a significant toll on Shiroshi.

He hadn't been openly depressed, but there had been odd moments when he'd appear to be brooding. Over the past three months, it had been a constant source of worry for Seiji.

All in all, if he's still able to smile, maybe he'll be okay.

When the three of them were together like this, murders and conspiracies seemed very far away… Even if their peace was only superficial and Hell was right below the floorboards.

Quickly sending his response, Shiroshi set his phone down on the table with a light *clunk*. "Now then, Seiji, it's time I told you about this as well. Do you remember Saori Toribeno?"

Now, there was a blast from the past.

Saori Toribeno was a writer for a monthly occult magazine, a story collector who ran a blog featuring scary stories and popular urban legends. The bitterness welling up in Seiji's chest was because her name reminded him of the first case he'd assisted with, ten months ago.

Satsuki Otose.

Satsuki had hounded a former lover into hanging himself, and when Shiroshi had exposed her crime, she'd been compelled to die the same way.

You reap what you sow. Ill begets ill. She'd brought it on herself.

Those sayings probably described her death pretty well, but a thought still haunted Seiji: Was he really all that different from her?

"Satsuki's former classmate, right? I'm pretty sure we only met her once…"

"She says she would like to meet again, this time for an interview. As a matter of fact, she hopes to publish the story in one of her books."

"Huh? An interview...? No way— About your proxy service for Hell?"

Bold, shocking headlines flashed through his mind:

Bone-Chilling Direct Interview: Hell's Proxy Service!

Twenty-Four Hours Shadowing the Punishment of the Damned!

...It would probably be one of those stories that ended with the writer's mysterious disappearance.

"No, no. It's *you* she wants to interview, Seiji. Not I."

"...Huh?"

"Let's see. Where should I begin?" Shiroshi murmured. He crossed his arms, thinking hard. "You remember that I submitted a scary story to her blog, don't you?"

"Huh? Yes. You said it was some random thing you made up to get an appointment with her."

"Heh-heh. Actually, the story went like this..."

It had been about the life of a young man.

When he was a child, a mirror fragment had gotten into his left eye. As a result, people who'd done wrong had begun to look like yokai to him. *Hyosube, dodomeki, aobouzu...* He'd disclosed countless sins with that eye. However, unable to use that power for the common good, he spent his days living in fear of the monsters lurking around him.

...Huh. That sounds weirdly familiar.

"Um, isn't that me?"

"Exactly. Since I was attempting to attract a ghost story professional, I thought my submission would need to seem fairly realistic."

Shiroshi sounded nonchalant, but in other words, he'd ripped off Seiji's story.

"Apparently, Ms. Toribeno thought it was true. Even after I confessed that I'd made it up, she continued to harbor doubts."

Hm. Had her professional instincts clued her in? You really couldn't underestimate such people.

"Why now, though? That was ten months ago."

"The other day, a journal of sorts was delivered to her editorial department. Like you, the journal's author could see others' sins in the form of yokai."

"…Huh?" That left Seiji speechless.

"This is a copy I had Ms. Toribeno send to me." Shiroshi took a manila envelope from Beniko, who'd been waiting beside him. Inside was a sheaf of several dozen sheets of paper. Judging from the ruled lines, Seiji figured the sheets must have been torn from a notebook. It appeared to be a diary at first glance, but the writer seemed to have added to it at random, whenever a thought occurred to them.

"The author's name is Mayuka Asaka. She's twenty-four years old. According to the journal, the change to her eye occurred eighteen years ago, just as yours did."

One day, she'd been looking up at a stray cat lounging on the branch of a tree in her family's garden when a sharp pain ran through her right eye. Something seemed to have fallen into it, but an examination by an ophthalmologist found no abnormalities… Except for the fact that, every so often, the people she saw with that eye changed into monsters.

"The first was a gardener her family employed. According to her, he looked like a fluttering length of cotton fabric."

"You mean…?"

"Yes, it was most likely an *ittan-momen*."

That was a yokai everybody knew from the *GeGeGe no Kitaro* series.

It was said to come flying out of nowhere into the road at night to wrap around the faces or necks of travelers and, in the worst-case scenario, suffocate them. It also kidnapped children, and there were regions where parents warned their kids that *ittan-momen* would come for them if they didn't hurry home at sundown.

"…The smell of crime was pretty strong on that one, huh?"

"Yes, in modern terms, an individual like that would be considered 'a suspicious character.'"

In fact, the gardener had later been arrested for targeting children on their way home from cram school. He'd wrapped a cloth around their necks on the road at night, choking them until they passed out, then dragged them into the shadows.

Both now and in the past, perverts were everywhere.

"The account bears a strong resemblance to the stories you told me, doesn't it?"

"Yes, well, you're right about that."

"As a result, Ms. Toribeno thought that my 'made-up story' might be true as well. That someone with an eye capable of disclosing others' sins might actually exist."

"Well, yeah, there's one right here."

Although he wasn't a fan of being talked about as though he were one of Nessie's pals.

"Heh-heh. At any rate, Ms. Toribeno promptly tried to get in touch with Mayuka, but…" Shiroshi held out a copy of a business card that had apparently been sent with the journal. Although Seiji had assumed it would have Mayuka's private contact information on it…

"Nine Echoes Lodge?"

"Yes, it's an inn run by her family; she works there as a hostess. When Ms. Toribeno called the telephone number on the card, a man who seemed to be the head clerk answered, then bluntly hung up on her."

Forget requesting an interview; he wouldn't even take a message.

Aha. So having hit a dead end with the interview she was really after, she'd contacted Shiroshi in the hopes of finding a breakthrough, at which point he'd promptly smooth-talked her out of all her information.

"For the moment, the question of whether we'll cooperate with the interview has been postponed. Ms. Toribeno's work seems to be keeping her quite busy, so why don't we pay Mayuka a visit first?"

"Huh? Us?"

"Yes, if she has an eye like yours, I'd like to meet her in person. You may stay home if you'd like, Seiji."

"N-no, of course I'll go with!"

Whoops. He'd jumped on that a little too fast.

"Heh-heh. So you are curious about her after all?"

"No, not particularly, but... Well, maybe a little."

In truth, he had another reason for wanting to go with Shiroshi. It wasn't important enough to mention, though, so he just nodded and fudged it. He also suspected that if he stayed behind, he might genuinely be left at a pet hotel...

"As a matter of fact, I've already made reservations at the inn on the business card. It seems to be near the border between Gifu and Nagano Prefecture."

"Meaning it's in Okuhida?"

"Yes. That area's famous for its hot spring villages, isn't it? Unfortunately, we won't be quite close enough to visit one."

The real question was, would the place have Hida beef?

"Wait— Then that's where the fragment of the Mirror of Illumination got into her eye?"

"Yes, she did say it happened in the garden of her house."

"But isn't that weird? My house was in Kanagawa."

One was on the eastern side of the country, the other in the center. Seiji had just assumed the mirror had broken way up in the sky, and the fragment that got into his eye had been carried on the wind. But in that case, the two places seemed a bit too distant. The thing couldn't possibly have exploded like a meteorite outside Earth's atmosphere and flown off in all directions, right?

"I believe there's a misunderstanding here. How do you suppose the fragments of the mirror came to fall from the sky, Seiji?"

"Huh? Well, um, I figured it burst in midair or something."

He was pretty sure a similar occurrence had happened in Hans Christian Andersen's "The Snow Queen."

"Heh-heh-heh. That's certainly easy to visualize, yes. However, while modern mirrors are made of glass, ancient mirrors were plates made of polished copper or bronze."

"Huh?"

Those words sparked a new connection in Seiji's mind: In the book of yokai pictures Shiroshi had shown him, the *ungaikyou*—the yokai version of the Mirror of Illumination—had been drawn as a round copper mirror.

"So, you see, it can't have shattered on its own. Someone intentionally destroyed it and sowed its fragments in the human world. Instead of the sky, it may have been done from the roof of a high-rise office or apartment building."

"B-but I was in a park near my house. We lived in a port town that had basically nothing; there weren't any buildings that tall—"

No… There *had* been something: a building there specifically *because* it was a port town with basically nothing.

"Actually, come to think of it, there was a decommissioned lighthouse nearby. During the day, anybody could go inside and look around."

"They must have scattered the pieces from there, then. The fragments were carried on the wind, and one found its way into your eye."

At Shiroshi's offhand remark, a wave of dizziness swept over Seiji. "So *the culprit* who scattered the mirror fragments is still out there somewhere?"

"Yes, that's right. Although I'm fairly certain I know who it is," Shiroshi said, casually showing off.

Seiji stared at him, shocked. He couldn't imagine even Shiroshi solving something this enormous so easily.

"The Mirror of Illumination is one of the magic mirrors handed down since antiquity, and there is a particular place in which it should be stored. An investigation will uncover the truth in due time. It's inevitable." Shiroshi shrugged; he was being rather evasive.

"Then who do you think—?" Seiji was planning to say *did it*, but he gulped and broke off. There was a chilling shadow in the depths of Shiroshi's eyes. It could have been anger, futility, irritation…or sadness.

"…Well. The one who made an attempt on my life in Nagasaki proved to be a close adviser to my father, Sanmoto Gorouzaemon. It's possible that there is a second traitor very close to me."

*

If someone were to ask me what I feared, I would answer, "Snakes and whistling."

I simply can't bear the sound of whistling on a dark path. In fact, I once heard a drunk whistling on the road at night and fainted on the spot.

Why? I really couldn't say. I often pestered Ranko, my father's second wife, to whistle for me when I was very young. It was a soft, clear sound that was sometimes unbearably lonely… And yet I developed a positive terror of it around the time my father died.

Oh, and then—snakes. Snakes that lie slickly across the road.

When I look back, this house seems to have a curious connection to snakes.

First, there's Kazutora. My father originally hired him so that we'd have male help, and he is an expert at catching snakes. I hear he takes pit vipers, starves them in a jar for a month, then preserves them in alcohol. I suppose, from the snakes' perspective, humans must be the truly dreadful ones.

Oh, how dreadful, how dreadful.

Does the voice in my memories belong to Mrs. Hatogaya, our former housekeeper? If I recall, that was the time Kazutora caught a rat snake that had made its home above the ceiling and cut it up while it was still alive.

"That man is a villain. Torturing the household god to death. Nothing could be more blasphemous."

With that same mouth, she'd speak ill of me. *Child of adultery, child of infidelity, cursed child.*

"That face of yours is a mark of the curse."

Oh, how dreadful, how dreadful.

After the death of my father, her employer, Mrs. Hatogaya never came to the house again. However, I remember that murmur of hers with every new season of snakes.

Oh, how dreadful, how dreadful.

Crimson the way ahead, crimson the path already trod. In this season, a red of suffocating intensity coils all around the house. Just like an enormous, bloodied serpent.

There's a rumor among the villagers that this house is cursed by snakes.

One snake was eaten, another bludgeoned to death, their corpses brutally exposed. They say this ominous red marks another realm colored by their remains, their entrails, and their blood.

They say that's why my father was killed.

The phantom attacker who killed him was a young man named Makito Kodokoro. Does that mean he was the snakes' avatar? —But only I know the names of those one truly ought to fear.

Ushioni and Nureonna.

*

True to pattern, this would be a trip for two.

Unfortunately, once again, Beniko had something else to do. She'd left the day before, so only the goldfish was there to see them off.

They boarded the Hokuriku Shinkansen at Tokyo Station, then transferred through several Japan Railway lines. After traveling for nearly half a day, they reached a local line that showed the name of the village they were bound for as its terminal station.

Maybe because it was a weekday afternoon, the train's old-fashioned, varnished wood interior was astonishingly empty. They had the car practically to themselves. Even in the other cars, most of the passengers were old folks who were obviously locals. If traffic was this sparse at the height of the fall foliage tourism season, this train line's future looked grim.

"It's too inconvenient to use as everyday transportation, really."

Apparently, there were only two trains per day. The end of service was surely imminent.

Thinking they'd enjoy the view from the window while they had the opportunity, Seiji and Shiroshi settled into a box seat.

In spite of themselves, they kept getting more keyed up, and they ended up breaking into the station box lunches they'd bought for dinner before the train was even moving. They compared the two, like food reporters on a travel program—*this is good, that could be better*—and managed to polish them both off before they knew it.

This wasn't how train journeys were supposed to be enjoyed, but after all, the thrill of travel did nothing to fill your stomach.

"My, we're off."

With a heavy *clunk*, the train's wheels began to turn. The houses outside the window grew sparse, and then all at once, the view changed from farming villages to mountains. A riot of colorful autumn leaves filled the window.

Before long, Shiroshi began to read, and Seiji found himself at loose ends. For no particular reason, his eyes fell on a certain object. "Hm? Come to think of it, you don't usually carry a tote bag, Shiroshi."

"Oh, this is a Shingen bag. I bought it so it would be easier to keep my phone with me."

According to him, it was basically a purse for guys. That made sense.

"Now then, while we're at it, perhaps we should discuss that journal." Closing his paperback, Shiroshi dexterously undid the bag's drawstring and took out the journal, which he'd folded in two. Yes, that bag seemed surprisingly handy.

Huh?

Seiji thought he'd glimpsed two small bottles inside the bag. Maybe Shiroshi had picked up something to drink.

"I gave you a portion of it earlier, Seiji. Have you read it through?"

"Oh, yes, technically. The person who wrote it was scared of snakes, just like me."

"It's a common fear. There's even a saying 'to loathe something as if it were a snake or a scorpion.'"

"It's supposed to be a holdover from back when people were monkeys, right? Because snakes were our only natural enemies up in the trees."

"Heh-heh. That's what they call an old wives' tale; you should take it with a grain of salt."

Careless Googling always landed Seiji in situations like this.

"Humans and snakes have coexisted for a very long time, probably since prehistory. From antiquity, while snakes have been an object of fear and loathing, they have simultaneously been worshipped as gods. One of the less common kanji characters for 'snake' can be read as *mi*, a sound used in the names of things considered holy or close to the gods in Japan."

Hm. Like in *mikoshi* and *miko*, the words for portable shrines and shrine maidens?

"Since snakes have no eyelids, they never blink. In addition, the way they shed their skins as they grow must have seemed particularly mystical and ominous to our distant ancestors. Awesome and awful, wicked yet sacred—that is the snake."

"Huh... I see." Seiji's personal hatred of snakes had been triggered by Mack the snake's dinnertime, so none of this was really clicking for him. "Speaking of that, didn't she also say she was scared of whistling?"

"Yes, whistling heard on the road at night. That may also be due to her fear of snakes, though."

"Huh? What do you mean?"

"There's an old superstition that whistling at night will summon a snake. Variants include 'a thief will break into your house' and 'a demon will appear.'"

So it was something along the lines of "If you cut your toenails at night, you won't be with your parents when they die."

"The ordinary character for 'snake' can also be read as *ja*, a sound with connotations of evil. In other words, whistling at night attracts bad things to you. To begin with, it's also a way to tell someone who's lurking in the darkness where you are."

Snakes or evildoers or demons... What exactly had she been afraid of?

"It may have been phantom slashers, you know," Shiroshi said significantly, holding out a copy of a newspaper article. It was dated sixteen years ago, and the headline read, *Man Stabbed to Death on Late-Night Road. Phantom Slasher?*

"Oh! The journal did say Mayuka's dad had been killed, didn't it?"

"Yes, this article is about that incident. There was a detailed account in a weekly magazine as well, and according to it..."

The victim's name had been Kuniomi Asaka. He'd been forty-four years old at the time, with an eight-year-old daughter.

"His corpse was found in front of a small *Jizo* shrine near his house at about one in the morning. He'd been stabbed to death. When his body was discovered, he'd only just passed away. The immediate cause of death was blood loss from a knife wound in his back, but since there were multiple contusions on his body as well, the theory was that he had been attacked with a bat, then stabbed to finish him off."

"Huh? How did they know the weapon was a bat?"

"The area had been plagued for the past six months or so by a random attacker who used a hard wooden bat. He'd exclusively targeted young women and the elderly. All were struck once from behind while on the road at night, and in every case, injuries were minor."

"Hm. So they assumed it was the same guy."

"On the night of the attack, a group of young men from the residents' association was out on patrol. The man who discovered the corpse belonged to the group on watch at the local guard station. As a result, they must have linked it to the other incidents."

"Um, if I recall, the culprit's name was—"

"Makito Kodokoro. Apparently, there were longstanding rumors that he was the phantom attacker."

"Was he that obviously suspicious?"

"He does seem to have been a problematic individual. He'd won multiple prizes in art contests as a student, and he was rather famous. However…"

In the end, maybe he'd only been a big fish in a very small pond. Although he should have sailed into a university of fine arts, he'd flunked the entrance exams spectacularly several years in a row. He'd opened a local art classroom, but it hadn't taken off. Around that time, he'd started to break things and let out weird shrieks and screams late at night, and he'd been reported to the police for it once or twice.

"He seems to have attacked a neighbor's pet dog with a bat as well."

At that level, he might as well have gone around advertising himself as the phantom attacker.

"As a result, when the members of the young men's group saw Kuniomi's corpse, they made an impetuous raid on Makito's house."

"…That doesn't sound very smart."

"This is a remote district, after all. The nearest police substation was on the other side of the mountain, so it's understandable that they tried to deal with the matter themselves. They really should have left it to the police, though."

"What did Makito do then?"

"He leaped from a second-floor balcony and fled barefoot into the mountains."

That seemed like a pretty bad move, too. By running off like that, he'd practically confessed to the murder.

"Later on, while they were discussing combing the mountain for him, they found his hanged corpse."

So it had ended in the worst possible way.

"…Was Makito really the killer?" asked Seiji.

If the accusation was false, no story could have been more dismal.

"He didn't leave a note, but when the young men's group searched his house, they found the knife used in the murder. It was still bloody; it had been wrapped in newspaper and thrown into the back of a closet. Later, DNA analysis confirmed that the blood's type matched Kuniomi's."

"So he was definitely the murderer, then." Seiji wasn't sure if *relief* was the right word for how he felt. It was an extremely complicated emotion.

"The bat was confiscated as well. No blood was found on it, but some hair was, and the DNA matched one of the phantom attacker's female victims."

In that case, there didn't seem to be any room for doubt.

"Yes, that was the police opinion as well. They declared the suspect dead when they sent the documents to the prosecutor."

"Um, but…" Driven by a sense that something wasn't quite right, Seiji interrupted. "The guy only went after old people and young women, didn't he? Isn't it weird that he'd attack Kuniomi?"

"My, that was a sharp observation. Particularly for you, Seiji."

Shiroshi reached out his right hand. Sensing an incoming head pat, Seiji tried dodging to the other side, but Shiroshi simply patted him with his left hand instead.

H-he's reading my moves.

"True, Kuniomi was a hundred and eighty centimeters tall, and he had advanced skills in judo."

"…If you were dumb enough to hit a guy like that, it seems likely you'd break your bat instead."

"He was a devout man, however: He always stopped to pray when he passed a *Jizo* shrine. On seeing Kuniomi worshipping at the shrine in traditional dress, the attacker may have mistaken him for one of the village's elderly residents."

Ah. That sounded plausible. Visibility would have been bad on the road at night.

"When he struck him, Makito discovered that his victim was a large man, far stronger than he was. At that point, he panicked. Fearing a counterattack, he beat Kuniomi violently with the bat, then stabbed him to death with a knife he carried for self-defense… That was the police opinion, at any rate."

Hm. It really didn't seem as if there was anything else unnatural about the case, but…

"Now, there are several points that concern me."

…There are, huh? Knew it.

"First, Makito's fingerprints weren't found on the knife." Shiroshi put up an index finger. "While that could mean he'd worn gloves during the attack, his previous victims all said that their assailant's hands were bare. The fact that his fingerprints were detected on the grip of the bat corroborates this."

"Um, maybe he wore gloves because it was cold that night or something?"

"Well, the incident occurred in May, you see. Not only that, but if gloves were used during the crime, a search of Makito's house failed to produce them."

"Could he have wiped off the prints when he got home, then?"

"That would mean he had carefully cleaned the hilt but left the blade covered in blood. That seems truly unnatural."

Hm. Now that he mentioned it—yes, it did.

"The second odd point is the fact that all the contusions were on the back of the corpse. That would mean Kuniomi kept his back turned to his assailant for the duration of the beating."

"That doesn't seem too weird, though… If he was trying to run away, he would have had to turn his back, wouldn't he?"

"Yes. However, all the blood at the scene was concentrated in one place. Kuniomi seems to have crouched in that spot the entire time, without attempting to escape, right up until he was stabbed."

"Huh?"

That *was* weird. Way too weird.

"Not only that, but there were no defensive wounds on the corpse. If attacked with a bat or a knife, one would ordinarily put out their hands to protect their face or torso, yet there wasn't a single cut on either of Kuniomi's hands."

Then instead of fighting back, protecting his face or body, trying to run, or calling for help, Kuniomi had just kept his back turned for the entire assault? That really *was*—

"You see? Strange, isn't it?"

"Yeah, extremely." Seiji nodded in wholehearted agreement—and then a question occurred to him. "Why was he walking around in the dead of night in the first place?"

The attack had happened at one in the morning, after all. In a town so rural that it didn't even have a decent convenience store, there couldn't be many places to go at that hour.

"It appears that his only daughter, Mayuka, had contracted an unseasonal case of influenza and was sick in bed, delirious with a high fever. He may have gone to worship at the shrine out of concern for her."

"…That's really tragic."

If he'd been murdered while praying for his child's recovery, it was a cruel world indeed.

"At the time of the incident, his second wife was at home, caring for Mayuka. Mayuka had been born to Kuniomi's first wife; Ranko was her stepmother. Kuniomi had remarried a year before the incident. At the time, he was forty-three and Ranko was nineteen."

"Huh?!" Seiji screeched, despite himself. An age difference of more than two decades? Seriously? "…Isn't that a little much?"

"Only the couple in question has a say in that sort of thing, really."

Well, yes, that was true.

"After Kuniomi's death, Ranko took custody of Mayuka. Since Mayuka is still helping her with the family business, their relationship seems to be positive."

Oh, good. The fact that the family he'd left behind was doing well would do more than anything to help the victim rest in peace.

"Actually, I'm not so sure of that."

"Huh?"

"As certain aspects of the incident remain a mystery, it's possible that the culprit was not the deceased Makito. The victim would hardly be able to pass on if the murderer were still at large."

"I—I mean, no, but…"

"Well, we'll investigate that in due time. After all, the journey's only just begun."

…Hang on. Things had taken a sharp turn toward "extremely unsettling."

"Um, you're talking as if we're going there for one of our usual Hell-related jobs, but that's not what this trip is about, is it?"

"That's a very good question. The answer will be something to look forward to once we arrive." Shiroshi gave an ominous little chuckle. Apparently, we were on Hell's version of a mystery tour. "Besides, our destination is also rumored to be a man-eating inn."

"Wh-what's that supposed to mean?"

"Heh-heh. That can be another surprise for later on."

Give me a break…

Seiji shuddered. As he fought the impulse to escape through the window, the train went through several tunnels of various sizes, crossed a railway bridge over a steep-walled valley, then powered its way up a slope. Finally, they reached a wooden station dyed bright red by the evening sun.

In any event, it seemed they'd arrived.

"That was quite a long journey, wasn't it?"

"It's weird how much traveling by train wears you out when you're just sitting the whole time."

After Seiji had hauled their luggage out onto the platform, the chilly autumn wind mussing up his already messy hair, he and Shiroshi both stretched. No other passengers had gotten off. There were no station employees in sight, either; it was probably an unmanned station.

"Well. If the address on the card is accurate, the inn should be behind the station."

"It's pretty unusual not to have a website these days. There weren't any reviews, even."

Chatting cheerfully, they crossed the tracks. The embankments were planted with silvergrass.

On the other side, they found a sloping road barely wide enough for one car. The cold wind was laced with the scent of damp, dead leaves. The unpaved road seemed rather like an animal trail, and it wound around like a snake.

As they walked along, side by side…

"Huh? Is that a shrine?"

The road had widened abruptly, and Seiji had spotted a small copper-roofed structure. When he peeked through the lattice into its gloomy interior, he saw a *Jizo* statue.

"I see. This must be the site of Kuniomi's murder."

"Huh? Here?"

There was a clear, empty space in front of the shrine. The ground was speckled with fallen leaves, and naturally, there was no chalk outline to show where the corpse had been.

Still, merely hearing that it was the sight of a murder made a chill run up Seiji's spine... This despite the fact that he was freeloading at a house that drew in killers left and right, of course.

"Umm, I'll go on ahead a bit."

As usual, Shiroshi had started busily examining the area. Turning away, Seiji hastily put some distance between himself and the shrine. As he walked up the hill alone, he came across a thin, cord-like item lying in the road.

It's probably a piece of rope, he thought. Only after he'd casually stepped over it did he realize what it really was.

A snake.

"Dwaaaaaaaaaah!"

He screamed and jumped, then screwed up his landing and came down on his rear. When he took another look, a gray-brown snake with a crooked chain of spots on its back was lying in a sinuous line on the sloping road.

Jesus.

"My, that's unusual. A snake bridge?"

Shiroshi had followed him at a leisurely pace. He leaped lightly over the snake—or so Seiji assumed, anyway. He was shaking with his eyes squeezed shut, so he couldn't see a thing.

"Heh-heh. A masterful display of spinelessness. I'd expect no less of you, but the sun will set on us if I stand here admiring the view. Let's vanquish the snake promptly, shall we?"

"...Uh, wait, 'admiring'?"

Ignoring Seiji's protest, Shiroshi picked up a branch. Using its tip to pin the snake's head, he caught it by the neck and relocated it to the tall grass. With that, the snake was summarily vanquished.

Th-thank goodness.

"Heh-heh-heh. Still, a snake on a mountain road is reminiscent of Kyoka Izumi's *The Saint of Mount Koya*, isn't it?"

That sounded familiar, in an extremely vague sort of way. "Um, he's an old author, right?"

"Yes, a literary giant who was active beginning in the 1890s. *The Saint of Mount Koya* is one of his early masterpieces. In the tale, Shucho—an

ascetic monk from Mount Koya—relates experiences he had while cross-
ing the mountains of Hida in his youth to a young man who's become his
traveling companion."

After struggling on bad roads crawling with snakes and leeches, Shucho
stays the night at an isolated dwelling deep in the mountains. However, the
house turns out to be the den of an enchantress who has the power to turn
men into beasts.

"In other words, without realizing it, Shucho had wandered into a world
that was not his own. And the threshold was a snake bridge."

Hm? What did he mean by *bridge*?

"Exactly like the situation we just encountered: A snake lay across his
path, blocking it, and he stepped over it. Snakes that lie across the road
serve as borders between this world and others. They're ill omens, but at
the same time, they're bridges that link the mortal realm with the realm of
the dead."

"Huh… So did we just cross into some other world back there?"

"Heh-heh. I suppose we may have, yes."

Come on, don't even joke about that.

"Still, the name 'Nine Echoes' brings a different work to mind." Something about the idea seemed to tug at Shiroshi, but then: "…No, I really
must be overthinking it. Never mind that; look." His arm came up to point
at something behind Seiji. "There's a snake back there as well."

"Yaugh!"

Another snake?! …But no, this time it was a signboard with a photo.

BEWARE OF AUTUMN PIT VIPERS.

The photo showed a coiled snake with a chain-like pattern running down
its thickset back. The more Seiji looked, the more it resembled the snake
they'd just evicted… *Wait. Pit vipers?*

"U-um, don't tell me—"

"Autumn pit vipers are aggressive and easily angered. Their venom is so
potent that even adults take six months to fully recover from it."

"Um, never mind that. Don't tell me the snake in the road was a pit
viper…"

"My, is that what it looked like?"

"Well, I mean, look. The chain on its back was just like the one in the photo."

"The lozenge pattern, yes. They do look similar, but ours was a young rat snake."

Huh? Seiji had run into rat snakes a few times back home, but they'd been plain, without any patterns on them. He thought he recalled them being thinner, too.

"Heh-heh. The juveniles don't look like the adults, you see. The eyes are probably the easiest way to distinguish between the two species. Pit vipers have slit pupils, while rat snakes have large, round ones."

True, the pit viper on the sign did look as mean as a yakuza spoiling for a fight. That said, if someone had asked Seiji whether rat snakes' eyes were round and cute, he would have shaken his head for all he was worth.

"Heh-heh-heh. They're docile and nonvenomous; you can even hold one on your arm once you're used to them. I hear they've recently become popular overseas as a variety of pet snake unique to Japan."

"Huh... Some people have weird tastes."

For now, he'd ignore the fact that *oni* with pet humans were probably less common than humans with pet snakes.

"Now, it will be dark before long. Let's go find lodgings of our own." Shiroshi pointed to the end of the sloping road, where a stone stairway split off like a grafted branch. The steps were made of uneven, natural stone, and above them...

"Whoa..."

A bright red canopy arched overhead. The stairs were flanked by rows of Japanese maples, and deep scarlet leaves spread above them like a procession of traditional paper umbrellas.

Keeping a wary eye out for an encore appearance by the snake, Seiji timidly made his way up the steps. At the top, they found a gate that could have belonged to a temple. Actually, the tranquil atmosphere did seem more suited to a temple or shrine than to an inn.

They passed through the gate together, and then...

Fire?

It was as if someone had snapped open a folding screen: The whole world was crimson.

What is that, a forest fire? he thought, startled. A moment later, he realized it was simply more maple trees, planted to fill the space between the property and the mountain behind it.

In front of them, a path as straight as the approach to a shrine ran from the gate to a solitary inn whose main entrance was set so high, it was equipped with a step. Something in its appearance did suggest a mountain temple, and yet in the midst of so many maples, it looked like a frog about to be swallowed by an enormous snake.

"I see. It's just as the journal said."

Shiroshi's words made a line from one of the pages surface in Seiji's mind: *Crimson the way ahead, crimson the path already trod.*

The whole area really was the color of blood—so intense, it was almost suffocating.

"I would imagine the 'season of snakes' refers to this time of year, when the autumn pit vipers appear."

"Do you think it gets this red every single year?"

"A good question. The trees appear to be mountain maples, but their coloring is strange."

Hm? How so?

"They're too red."

Seiji had to agree with that. This red was practically the color of fresh blood, or of fire.

"Anthocyanins, which lend color to the leaves, are produced by sunlight and cold nighttime temperatures. As a result, varying amounts of sun exposure mean that even a single tree will have different hues in different areas."

Come to think of it, it was pretty rare to see a tree that was solid red. They usually had yellow or orange gradations here and there.

"B-but then… What's up with this place?"

"I couldn't say. Perhaps it really is another world," Shiroshi joked, shrugging.

When things got this surreal, it hardly mattered how photogenic the scenery was.

Still, I guess I'll get a picture.

Taking his phone out of his back pocket, Seiji spotted two words on the screen: *No Service.*

"Huh? There's no cell reception here."

"My, I don't have a signal, either."

Seiji tried holding his phone at different heights and angles, but it didn't change anything. He seemed to remember hearing that everywhere except extremely remote areas had cell service these days, but…

"Heh-heh-heh. An isolated lodge in another world in the mountains. This is becoming more and more the realm of Kyoka Izumi."

"…Please just stop."

"Ah. It appears there's an enchantress as well."

A woman had appeared on the smooth white gravel of the front courtyard. Her kimono was almost black, and her obi was a deep gray; she could have been in mourning dress. Granted, if you ignored the details, Shiroshi probably looked as if he were wearing a burial kimono.

Just then…

…a red stain bloomed on Shiroshi's chest.

It looked like a palm print, and Seiji did a double take. However, when Shiroshi plucked it off, it turned out to be a red leaf no bigger than the tip of his thumb.

It resembled a tiny, bloodstained hand. Shiroshi twirled it between his fingertips, then pressed it to his lips.

"Now then, what horror will present itself? Will it be an *oni* or a snake? It could even be both."

*

Seiji's very first thought was, *They're honey-colored.*

The woman's eyes were amber, the color of nectar. She bowed politely. "Master Shiroshi Saijou and his companion, correct? Thank you for coming such a long distance to stay with us. My name is Mayuka Asaka. I will be serving you today."

That drew a startled, involuntary noise from Seiji. *Then she's the one...*

So this was the writer of that journal, the one with the shard of the Mirror of Illumination in her eye?

The longer he looked at her, the more she appeared to be an ideal Japanese beauty. Her nose was perfectly straight, and her lips were thin and taut. Beneath her glossy, upswept black hair, the nape of her neck seemed more delicate than a waxwork doll's.

"A room in a detached cottage has been prepared for you. I'll show you to it in a moment."

They followed Mayuka up a flagstone path. Whoever swept the white gravel courtyard clean must have been positively neurotic: There wasn't a single fallen leaf in sight.

The high-set main entrance with its elegant step would have been right at home in a distinguished traditional house. In fact, it more closely resembled a head priest's quarters like the kind Seiji sometimes saw in travel programs about temple guesthouses.

After filling out the place's guest book in a wood-floored room containing the reception desk, they set off for the cottage.

With Mayuka in the lead, they made their way down a covered connecting walkway. The property was on an incline, and their path was frequently interrupted by small stairways. It seemed a bit like a maze.

"It's very quiet. Where are your other employees?" asked Shiroshi.

"My mother and I make do by ourselves for the most part, though we employ a man to serve as our head clerk."

He must have been the one who kept hanging up on Saori's requests for appointments.

"And where is the proprietress now?"

"Actually..." Mayuka hesitated. "She passed away this morning."

For a moment, Seiji didn't understand what he'd just heard. Even Shiroshi was speechless.

"My mother had a congenital heart condition, you see. She took medication to lower her blood pressure every evening. She had surgery the year before last, but the prognosis was unfavorable."

"My deepest condolences on your loss. Did she pass away at the hospital?"

"…No, here."

Yikes.

"Her health had seemed poor for the past several days. She went to bed early last night, and she never woke. Her physician said it was most likely acute heart failure."

"When will you hold the funeral?"

"Unfortunately, today was an inauspicious day, so the wake will be tomorrow."

Even if it was just a matter of luck, they'd chosen an awful time to barge in on her. She had to have a ton of other things to do right now, such as making funeral arrangements…

"Things will be lonely from now on, won't they?" Shiroshi observed, just to say something.

Mayuka gave a small nod. "She was more than a mother to me. She was my elder sister, my friend, and—" Before she could finish, they reached the cottage. "Here is your room."

She opened the sliding door to reveal a wood-floored antechamber, with a tatami room about thirteen square meters beyond it. In its center, two legless chairs faced each other across a low ebony table. There was an ornamental alcove and a closet, but Seiji didn't see the TV, refrigerator, or safe for valuables typical of inns.

And…

"Oh-ho, this is quite something." Shiroshi made a low, appreciative noise that sounded a bit like the call of an owl.

At the very back of the room, there was a set of paper-and-wood sliding doors whose lower halves were set with glass panes. The view through the glass was a dazzling deep red.

Autumn leaves and the last light of evening.

Seiji felt drawn to the window. When he went closer, he saw a mountain stream so near, it looked as if he could reach out and touch it. He could hear the water's murmur. Its perfectly clear, mirrorlike surface was ablaze with the twilight sky and the scarlet leaves of the trees on its banks.

"The view is too uncanny to be magnificent. Frankly, I find it profoundly unsettling."

"Huh?" Startled, Seiji looked at Shiroshi. The boy's profile was unexpectedly serious; his eyes were fixed on the water's surface. "Um, why—?"

But before Seiji could ask what he meant...

"What brought you to this inn?" At the sound of Mayuka's voice, they turned. She'd paused in the act of preparing tea. "It just seems odd. This area has no sightseeing spots to speak of. I thought you might be students on a tour of secluded railway stations, but neither of you seem to be train enthusiasts." Her face was a little tense; the suspicion she felt was creeping into her expression.

And then...

"I'm sorry to trouble you when you're working, but may I speak with you for a few minutes?" Briskly seating himself in one of the legless chairs, Shiroshi motioned for the bewildered Mayuka to take the place across from him. Naturally, Seiji planted his butt on the tatami like some big, awkward art object.

"Mayuka, are you acquainted with a woman named Saori Toribeno? She's active as a writer of scary stories in Tokyo."

"...No, I've never heard of her."

"The other day, I'm told she received this journal by mail. The enclosed business card seemed to identify you as the sender." As he spoke, Shiroshi drew the folded journal out of his Shingen bag.

When Mayuka took it, her eyes widened in shock. She clearly recognized it. "This is... Yes, I did write this. It's just a series of autobiographical essays I scribbled down as a diversion, though. It isn't the sort of thing I could show others."

"The content is true, then?"

The woman stifled a gasp, but before she could deny it, Shiroshi gestured to Seiji. "You see, he has an eye like yours."

"What?" Mayuka murmured. From her face, it seemed he'd caught her completely off guard.

"A mirror fragment found its way into his left eye. He says that, ever since, he's seen people who've committed sins as yokai."

"...He sees them, too?"

Her amber eyes focused on Seiji. They were bewitching and so beautiful that they made him flinch.

"Then it's as I thought. You're the same, aren't you, Mayuka?"

Realizing she'd slipped, Mayuka startled. Then she shook her head. "N-no, I don't know what you mean. Please excuse me; I have many things to do." She started to get to her feet.

"Don't you want to know the truth of your father's death?"

Mayuka froze as if he'd struck her. "...Are you with the police?"

"No." Shaking his head, Shiroshi took a business card from the front of his kimono. "As it happens, 'Shiroshi Saijou' is a false name. I run a detective agency in Tokyo *under the name 'Odoro Rindou.'* This is Seiji, my assistant."

...Wait.

Hold it, hang on a second. What did he just say?

"Well, at a first meeting, I thought 'assistant' would be the easiest title to understand."

"No, no, no, not that part!" Seiji's voice cracked; he was almost in tears.

Countering with a smile, Shiroshi put a finger to his lips. *Shh.* Catching himself and shutting up fast, Seiji stole a glance at Mayuka. Sure enough, she was holding a terribly familiar business card. Self-important gold letters spelled out *Rindou Detective Agency* on a black background.

The name beneath them was "*Odoro Rindou.*"

Th-that little— Now he's done it!

Fighting the impulse to start swearing, Seiji felt himself break out in a cold, clammy sweat. In all probability, Beniko had forged that card. This was clearly fraud... And if Odoro found out, there would be one hell of a bloodbath.

Odoro Rindou was an extremely sharp private detective known among the public as the "Detective Who Summons Death." He was actually the son and heir of the other demon king, Shinno Akugorou. Like Shiroshi, he ran a proxy service for Hell.

To Seiji, he seemed like a sorry excuse for a person; nothing but tyranny and snobbishness walking around in a pretentious suit. Was it his imagination, though, or had Shiroshi been unilaterally dumping the guy into nasty situations lately?

As expected…

"Odoro Rindou… It can't be. Do you mean *the*…?"

…the business card was tremendously effective.

Mayuka lowered her gaze for a few moments. When she looked back up at Shiroshi, the "famous detective," the emotion in her eyes was something between bewilderment and awe.

"If you don't mind, I'd like to ask you a few questions, just for reference," he said. "I'm told the first person to discover the body was one of the young men keeping watch that night. Was he acquainted with Kuniomi?"

"…It was Kazutora Sawada. He'd been hired as live-in help about half a year before the incident. In addition to doing the harder physical tasks, I'm told he organized my father's library. He still works here as our head clerk."

According to Mayuka, the young men's group had done night patrols about twice a week. They'd been in the habit of holding a drunken party after returning to the guardroom, though they called this, too, "being on night watch."

On the day of the incident, Kazutora had left the party early and had found Kuniomi's corpse on his way home. Shaken, he'd run back to the guardroom.

Aha. So that reckless raid was partially fueled by alcohol.

"What sort of person was your departed father to you?"

Mayuka looked down again. The shadows of her eyelashes, cast across her pale cheeks, trembled eloquently. "My father was a scholar of local history." Even so, her voice was cold and flat. "He may have been an amateur, but he was extremely dedicated to his research. He spent all day in a storehouse he'd converted into a study. It didn't matter how much I tried to talk to him; he kept his back to me and never responded."

"...Did you ever resent him?"

"Frankly, I did as a child. I wasn't even sure whether my father truly considered me his daughter. However..." Pausing for a moment, Mayuka drew a hesitant breath. "My father's previous wife—my mother—was an arranged match forced on him by his relatives. Perhaps it was the same for her. Soon after I was born, she ran off with a man she'd been seeing. Granted, it may have been me she disliked."

Her smile might have been wry if it wasn't so sad.

"It made my father the laughingstock of the whole village. People called him a fool of a scholar whose young wife had run out on him, forcing him to keep the child she'd made with another man."

So Kuniomi wasn't actually Mayuka's father—or, at least, the people around them had assumed as much.

"My father's relatives pushed him to have my DNA tested at once and to get rid of me, but he wouldn't. He didn't really talk to me. He never even held my hand. Still, he stayed my father."

"...And you feel that was his way of showing affection?"

"I think he was simply a clumsy person."

In a motion as smooth as flowing water, Mayuka bowed, then rose to her feet. "There's nothing more I can tell you. My father died sixteen years ago. It's the distant past for me, though the gossiping villagers seem to feel it was only yesterday. To be honest, I would prefer the matter be left alone."

Just as she turned to leave...

"May I ask one last question?"

"...Go ahead."

"Who were Ushioni and Nureonna?"

There was no answer. After wordlessly opening the sliding door, Mayuka crossed into the antechamber. "Please make yourselves at home."

Then she closed the door without a sound.

"She's quite a formidable opponent." As the woman's footsteps faded away, Shiroshi sighed.

"So what do we do now?"

"We planned to spend the night in any case. We'll watch for another opportunity and try again."

In other words, it seemed they'd gone to all this trouble for nothing. Then again, taking Mayuka's feelings into account, Seiji didn't think it was a good idea to pry any further.

"Since we're here, let's consider it a hot spring trip and make the most of it. There's still time before dinner; why don't you go take a bath?"

"Huh? What about you?"

"Now that we've heard from Mayuka, I'd like to organize what we know. It feels as if I'll have a theory soon." He began to flip through the journal, which Mayuka had left on the table.

Um, since we came all the way here, why don't we go together? Frankly, I bet there are more snakes out there... The words were on the tip of Seiji's tongue, but Shiroshi's profile looked so intent that Seiji thought better of it and kept quiet. It seemed like a shame to disturb him.

Changing into a yukata provided by the inn, he trudged out of the cottage.

It should have been just past sunset, but it was already fully dark outside, and the hush seemed to be creeping up behind him on stealthy feet. Feeling isolated and uneasy, Seiji had started whistling to cheer himself up, when...

If you whistle at night, you'll summon a snake.

Feeling as if he'd heard Shiroshi's voice, he flinched and stopped in his tracks. He looked around fearfully, but there were no signs of a snake popping out to say hello. His relief didn't last long, though.

"Huh...? Where am I?"

This was ridiculous. Nobody could get lost in a connecting walkway.

And yet...the incandescent lights glowing overhead seemed somehow cold and unreliable. The frequent turns and flights of stairs made for surprisingly bad visibility. If the path had forked at some point, he might have walked right past it.

The wood grain on the railing seemed oddly vivid, and when Seiji spotted red leaves beyond it, he felt as if he'd stumbled onto a bloody corpse on a dark road. The night wind blew, rustling the trees. It sent a shiver through him, and then...

Hm?

What was it? A feeling that something was off tugged at a corner of his mind. He couldn't pinpoint what was causing it, though, and he hurried away, as if fleeing from the red of the leaves.

Something's wrong with the maples on this mountain.

It was as if they were growing redder as the hour grew later and the darkness, deeper.

"...Huh? Wait, what?"

Finding himself abruptly facing something unexpected, Seiji stopped, taken aback.

He'd just assumed the walkway was heading toward the main house, but it had led him to an attached storehouse instead. The plaster-covered doors were standing wide open. Was somebody in there?

"G-good evening...," Seiji called timidly, peeking inside.

The interior was a tatami room about thirteen square meters in area. The walls on either side were lined with bookshelves. This was probably the study where Kuniomi had lost himself in research.

In the very back, there was a folding screen decorated with a painting of crashing waves and a high latticed window meant to let in light. The moonlight filtering in threw faint shadows onto the tatami.

Huh? Behind that screen...

Seiji had wandered a few steps closer, but what he glimpsed beyond the screen's edge made him stop in his tracks. Candlesticks and incense on a stand of unvarnished wood—a funeral altar, meant to be placed by the head of the deceased.

In other words...

Either Ranko's body or the coffin in which she would be laid to rest was behind that screen.

"U-um... I'm sorry to have disturbed you."

The mere thought that there was a corpse right in front of him made

Seiji break out in gooseflesh. More than ready to run for it, he bowed to
the unseen coffin, then hastily turned on his heel.

But then—

Clatter.

The noise had come from behind him, and he flinched and froze. Fearfully and so stiffly, the joints in his neck seemed to creak, he looked back.

The next moment…

…with the force of a sudden inferno, the shadow of a huge snake reared
up from the other side of the screen and lunged at him.

"Eeeeeep!"

Seiji screamed, cringing away and staggering backward. Then the snake's
shadow vanished as abruptly as a blown-out candle flame.

"Waugh!"

Seiji's back collided with something, and he almost shrieked again.

When he turned around, he saw a mummy. That was really the only
way to describe the figure. From its size, it appeared to be a middle-aged
man of middling height and medium build, but there were bandages
wrapped all around his head and a thick gauze pad at the back of his neck.
He was wearing a short traditional coat with the inn's symbol on it, so he
was probably on the staff, but—

Could he be…?

Was this Kazutora Sawada?

The strangest thing about the man were his eyes. They peered out from
between the bandages, so unfocused that he might have been a sleepwalker.
It was impossible to tell where he was looking. Could he even see Seiji standing there?

"…Um, are you all right?" Seiji asked reflexively. Then he saw the rope-
like object in the man's hand, and his eyes went wide with shock.

Was that a rat snake? It wasn't a juvenile, apparently; there was no lozenge pattern on its blue-gray body. When he looked closer, he realized its
head had been cut off. And yet it seemed almost as if the headless snake
were still alive— Or was it? What terrifying vitality.

Then Seiji heard a weird cough.

As if he were hocking a loogie, the man spat something out.

It was a bone.

No. No way, he can't have…

Seiji gulped. He'd noticed that the surface of the snake's severed neck was weirdly uneven. Almost as if human teeth had chewed through it.

Don't tell me he bit the head off a live snake.

Seiji shuddered. In the back of his mind, an alarm began to sound.

Get moving. Run.

He backed away carefully, as if he were staring down a bear. Slowly, slowly. Two steps, three. As he gradually widened the distance between them…

"Huh?"

…he blinked, and in that moment, the man turned into an *oni* as big and rugged as a boulder. No, that wasn't quite right. It wasn't just an *oni*. It had the head of a bull.

Fierce horns sprouted from its forehead. Its blazing eyes glared at Seiji, and a steady trickle of saliva dripped from its fang-lined mouth.

Then, slowly, it raised its left hand to its jaws and took another big bite of the snake.

"YaaaaaaaaaaAAAAaaaaaugh!"

With the world's most pathetic scream, Seiji scrambled out of the storehouse.

✳

"Getting lost and encountering corpses seems to be your specialty, Seiji."

When Seiji burst into the cottage and delivered a tearful, frantic description of what he'd seen in the storehouse, those were the first words out of Shiroshi's mouth. He seemed to feel them keenly. "Well, to be honest, I did have a feeling this would happen."

"Then you should have stopped me!" Seiji howled.

Shiroshi patted his head soothingly. "Still, eating a live snake… That sounds quite unsafe."

"It really does, doesn't it? It sure didn't look very tasty, either."

"Heh-heh-heh. In that case, a meal may not have been what he was after. He may have been trying to break a curse."

What is that supposed to mean?

"Since antiquity, eating a snake has been considered an effective way to quell its curse. Eating the life you've taken is both a memorial to the deceased and a ceremony to lay their soul to rest. If you kill it and eat it, you won't be cursed. Conversely, there are more than a few tales of those who refused to partake and were cursed to death."

Gobbling your victim up for dinner seemed more sinful to Seiji, but maybe it was the same as eating your catch when you went fishing.

"So, uh... You're saying Kazutora's been cursed by a snake, and he was eating one whole in an attempt to undo it?"

"Well, the possibility does exist, but he may also simply have lost his mind."

"Um, I've got a really bad feeling about this. I think we should leave the inn, fast."

"I agree. We'll have a difficult time leaving the village before dawn breaks, though. And if worse comes to worst, I can use the yokai under my father's command, so I don't think anything truly disastrous will happen."

So he plans to use them like an ultra-vicious personal security company? Human or supernatural, influential parents were a really handy thing to have.

"Huh? Wait, so if something happens when I'm by myself, I'll just have to accept death?"

"No, erm... Heh-heh-heh-heh-heh."

He dodged the question!

"Now then, since you've returned, shall we review the incident? I think I'm quite close to uncovering the truth behind Kuniomi's murder."

"Say what?!"

For detective work, that was way too fast.

Seiji's thoughts must have shown on his face; Shiroshi cleared his throat. "I won't deny that it's still firmly in the realm of speculation, but I don't think I'm entirely off the mark, either."

Apparently, what had clinched it for him were the two yokai Seiji had seen in the storehouse. The man he assumed was Kazutora, the head clerk, had been Ushioni. Ranko, who'd been lying in her coffin, had been—

Let's see… Huh? What yokai was it again?

Its silhouette had definitely looked like a snake's. However, since it had mostly been hidden behind the screen, the details had escaped him.

"W-wait just a second!"

Rummaging through his bag, Seiji pulled out a large art book. He turned his back to hide it like a middle schooler peeking at his crib sheet during a test and was flipping through its pages, when—

"My, the Toriyama Sekien collection?"

"Eep!"

Shiroshi had peeked over his shoulder and called it in one.

"You brought that all the way from the study at home? I'm impressed; it must have been heavy—" He whisked the book out of Seiji's hands and opened the back cover, and his voice broke off abruptly. His eyes were focused on a note scribbled in pencil on the copyright page: *Water stains, yellowing, 2,000 yen.* "…Did you buy this at a used bookstore, Seiji?"

B-busted!

"Um, I just happened to see it at Book-Off the other day…"

"I see. There's actually a smaller paperback version of this same book that may be purchased new at ordinary bookstores."

"You're kidding! I looked everywhere because I heard it was out of print!"

By the time he thought, *Oh crud*, it was too late. Giving up, Seiji drooped like a dog with its tail between its legs. "Um, I thought if I studied that book, I might get a little better."

In short, he'd been doing some independent learning. He was well aware that there was no need to hide such activities, but…

It does seem kinda presumptuous, or like I'm getting full of myself, or something.

After all, it was the first time Seiji had ever considered trying to be useful to somebody.

On that island in Nagasaki, Shiroshi had been kind enough to say he'd believe what Seiji saw. If he was going to be Shiroshi's eyes, Seiji had to have as much confidence in his own judgment as possible. He'd thought that learning about yokai would be a good start.

Maybe he couldn't do the sort of thinking Shiroshi did, but if he could at least learn—if he could do that, he'd thought he might manage to be a little bit useful. Like a real assistant.

Not that he could ever tell Shiroshi that.

"Heh-heh-heh-heh-heh."

Shiroshi abruptly burst into creepy laughter. Then he ruffled Seiji's wavy hair vigorously, so that it stuck out crazily in all directions. "My, that's no good," he said, before combing it back down with his fingers. Then…

"Starting next month, I'll add money for books to your regular allowance. I'd advise beginning with three per month; there's no need to push yourself. Once we're home again, I'll show you a few that I recommend."

You've got to be kidding me. He saw through all of it! Trembling with shame, Seiji was fighting the urge to crawl under the low table and hide, when…

"Now, then." Clearing his throat, Shiroshi began paging through the art book. "What you saw in the storehouse was definitely 'something like a snake,' yes?"

"Oh, yes. It's just that I didn't get a really good look at it…"

"Hmm. If it was with an *ushioni*, I really do suspect it was a *nureonna*."

Why was he treating them like a set?

"Although most yokai appear independently, there are a few that are seen in pairs. *Shitanaga-uba* and *shunobon*, for example. *Ushioni* and *nureonna* are a particularly notorious combination."

Shiroshi opened the book to a certain page and showed it to him.

Nureonna, the caption said.

It was basically a snake with a human head. However, the face was that of a young woman; the hair was long and very black, and it seemed somehow lewd.

Wait… Huh?

This didn't feel quite right. What was it? Something was tugging at a corner of his mind.

"Um, what sort of yokai is a *nureonna*?"

"According to one theory, they're the yokai incarnation of sea snakes. They sometimes assume human form, but their hair is always soaking wet. That's how they acquired their name."

"And, uh, why are they a set with *ushioni*?"

"I'll explain that next."

He turned the art book's pages again, opening to one in *The Illustrated Demon Horde's Night Parade*, the same section as the *nureonna*.

This one had long, sharp claws and ominously fierce horns. All of the thing's facial features were vaguely oxlike, but its hairy body reminded Seiji of a spider.

The name beside the picture was "*Ushioni*."

"Now then, this is an *ushioni*. It's a yokai that lives near water; by waterfalls, deep pools, or the ocean. As you saw, Seiji, it can have the face of an ox and the body of an *oni*, but it may also be the other way around."

"Huh... I see. So it's based on a cow? That doesn't seem very scary."

"And yet in *The Pillow Book*, Sei Shonagon lists *ushioni* as one of her 'Things Whose Very Names Frighten Me.'"

"Huh? You mean people have been scared of these things since way back then?"

"That's right. Precisely because oxen were used to till fields, transport cargo, and quite literally worked as beasts of burden, the idea that the positions of oxen and humans could be reversed terrified the people of the Middle Ages. That is why they merged an ox with an *oni*. Both had horns in common, too."

Hm. What a guilt-ridden story.

"It was a legend of the Sanin region that paired *ushioni* with *nureonna*. According to that tale..."

A man was walking by the sea when a woman who was drenched from head to toe appeared and asked him to hold her infant. When he took it in his arms, the woman disappeared into the ocean.

The next thing he knew, the baby grew as heavy as a stone, and then an *ushioni* appeared and gored him to death.

"That's one vicious team play."

"If we reframe it as a modern crime, the *ushioni* would be the actual murderer, and the *nureonna* the accomplice who set the stage."

So if they applied that to Kuniomi's murder... "You mean Kazutora was the killer, and Ranko the accomplice?"

"Yes, while Makito becomes a victim the pair pinned their crime on."

And if they went further and applied the legend itself to the situation...

"The incident can be summarized as follows: As a *nureonna*, Ranko gave Kuniomi an infant to hold. Then Kazutora took the role of the *ushioni* and gored him to death with his horns—in other words, he stabbed him with his knife."

And indeed, after being badly beaten with a bat, Kuniomi had been stabbed to death.

"If we take that as our premise, it would provide an explanation for the remaining mysteries with regard to Kuniomi's corpse."

"Meaning...?"

"First is the lack of defensive wounds. Second is the way the contusions were concentrated on his back. Those two things mean that, while the killer was beating him with a bat, Kuniomi didn't try to run, nor did he attempt to use his hands to protect himself. He simply crouched there with his back to his assailant."

Yeah, that's weird no matter how you look at it.

"However, if you think of it this way, it's quite natural: During the attack, Kuniomi was unable to strike back at his attacker or shield himself because his hands were full. In short, he was holding something that he would have given his life to protect."

...Wait.

Wait just a minute, it can't be...

"Yes. *Mayuka.* To begin with, a *nureonna* is a yokai who *makes her victim hold a sleeping child.* Kuniomi was holding Mayuka, who was insensible with a high fever."

Mayuka, who'd been eight years old at the time, had come down with an unseasonal case of the flu. Her stepmother, Ranko, had been the one caring for her through the night. As both a father and a husband, Kuniomi had been there as well.

"Everything from this point on is conjecture, but…" Shiroshi raised an index finger. "First, Ranko lured Kuniomi to the *Jizo* shrine sometime after midnight. Kuniomi was carrying his only daughter, who was ill. The simplest possibility is that Ranko told him she wanted to take Mayuka to the emergency room. At the time, a phantom attacker was haunting the area and Kazutora was away, so it would have been the perfect excuse to get Kuniomi to accompany her."

Then Ranko walked down the hill road with the other two. She might have given Mayuka sleeping pills earlier, to make sure she didn't wake up.

Before long, the trio came to the *Jizo* shrine. Kuniomi was in the habit of worshipping there, and he probably stopped. With Mayuka in his arms, he bowed to the object behind the lattice, and just then…

"Kuniomi spotted *a certain thing*. When Ranko saw this, she whistled a signal—and Kazutora leaped out, caught up a bat he'd hidden in advance, and struck at Kuniomi."

"Um, what was the thing?"

"Most likely a juvenile rat snake. Kazutora was an expert at catching snakes; he'd trapped one beforehand, weakened it, and laid it in front of the shrine."

"Huh? What for?"

"In order to make Kuniomi think there was a pit viper at his feet."

Right. Young rat snakes looked similar to poisonous pit vipers. On a dark road at night, it wouldn't have been possible to tell them apart.

"That's why Kuniomi couldn't set Mayuka down and fight back, or even run away. If his assailant gave chase and he dropped her, she might have been bitten."

Even full-grown adults took several months to recover from pit viper venom. For a young child, especially one who'd been weakened by a fever, it could easily have been fatal.

"B-but the snake at his feet and the whistled signal… How could you know about those? There's no way to prove either of them."

"Mayuka's journal. According to it, she has an unnatural fear of 'snakes that lie across the road' and 'whistling heard on the road at night.' In addition, it says she developed an absolute terror of these things around the time Kuniomi died."

Oh, I see. If her phobias were caused by trauma from the incident…

"When the crime occurred, Mayuka was mostly unconscious. As a result, the aftereffects of the incident lingered as subconscious trauma. The snake in front of the *Jizo* shrine, the whistled signal that precipitated the attack— her fear of those things ate away at her heart."

To Mayuka, both things had become linked to her father's murder—to the death of Kuniomi, who'd held her close, shielding her with his back, protecting her to the end.

So the odd state of the corpse was because it belonged to a father who'd been holding his child, someone he'd had to protect even if it cost him his life.

"Kazutora beat Kuniomi mercilessly, then stabbed him to death. From the fact that he chose a wooden bat as one of his weapons, he probably intended to pin the crime on Makito all along. If he left clear evidence that the victim had been beaten with a bat, it would inevitably be linked to the phantom attacker."

In fact, that was exactly what had happened.

"Ranko carried the sleeping Mayuka back home, disposed of the bat, and continued to care for the girl as if nothing had happened. Meanwhile, Kazutora wrapped the bloody knife in newspaper, concealed it in his coat, then ran back to the guardroom and the young men's group."

After that, he spurred on the members of the group, who were already drunk and more than ready to start some trouble. They forced their way into Makito's house and began to search it.

"During the search, Kazutora hid the newspaper-wrapped bundle in the closet, then 'discovered' it in the presence of his companions. Even if his fingerprints were detected on the paper, if he were part of the group who'd found it, he wouldn't need to fear being questioned by the police."

"S-so Makito was framed? Then why would he kill himself over…?" But before Seiji even finished his question, it hit him: Makito's suicide probably hadn't been triggered by Kuniomi's murder.

"That's right. It was because of the phantom attacker incidents. Since Makito actually *was* behind those, when he saw the angry young men's group, he assumed they had come to apprehend him for that."

In other words, Makito hadn't even known about Kuniomi's death, or that he'd been framed for his murder. He'd killed himself simply because he'd feared being arrested for assault.

"I don't think the criminals could have predicted Makito's suicide. However, it was extremely convenient for them. After all, dead men tell no tales."

In the end, this crime had killed two people. One was the direct victim, Kuniomi. The second was Makito, who'd been hounded into killing himself by being set up as the suspect.

"But why would they do something so awful?" Seiji's voice was hoarse.

"Well…" Shiroshi tilted his head. "If we may indulge in vulgar conjectures, the situation might have been similar to that of Mayuka's birth mother. Disgusted by her marriage to a much older man, Ranko may have entered into an intimate relationship with the live-in hired hand, who then conspired with her to kill her husband. If she took custody of Mayuka after that, they could swindle her out of her inheritance as well."

It was hopelessly cruel. For that reason, though, it was easy to understand.

"Conversely, Mayuka is an enigma. Her eye must have seen the two as an *ushioni* and a *nureonna*. It would have been clear to her who had really murdered her father. And yet…"

Exactly. She'd continued to live as family with the ones who were responsible for her father's death.

And that wasn't all…

"She was more than a mother to me. She was my elder sister, my friend, and—"

It was impossible to reconcile the fact that Ranko had killed Kuniomi with the deep affection Mayuka had felt for her.

As if telling a secret, Shiroshi abruptly lowered his voice. "As a matter of fact, I heard a rather unsavory rumor. It sounds as if Mayuka may have been abusing the power of the Mirror of Illumination."

"Huh? No, that can't be right… Is that even possible?"

How, exactly?

In the first place, the Mirror of Illumination was a magic mirror with the power to reveal sins. You could use it for the good of the world and mankind, but it didn't seem as if there was much else to do with it.

"Heh-heh-heh. You *would* say that, Seiji." Sounding weirdly pleased, Shiroshi patted his head appreciatively. Had he gone nuts or something? "The fact that the Mirror of Illumination discloses others' sins means that it grants the user the power of life and death over others by revealing their weaknesses—the kind of secrets that, if exposed, would spell certain destruction. In other words, Seiji, that eye of yours is *a perfect tool for blackmail*."

"…Huh?"

Blackmail—that thing where you threaten someone into paying you not to talk?

"Now, deviating from the main subject slightly, there's a story circulating on the internet known as 'The Man-Eating Inn.'"

With that preamble, Shiroshi began to relate a questionable urban legend along the lines of "The Detective Who Summons Death."

Several years ago, on an introduction from a certain man, an up-and-coming actress stayed at a certain inn deep in the mountains. During her stay, a young girl who wasn't quite human or demon appeared, pointed at her, and said "Ubagabi."

Two weeks later, the actress received a threatening letter describing her secret sin.

She'd once had an elderly neighbor who habitually stole her kerosene.

Fed up with this behavior, the actress had switched the contents of the container for gasoline. She'd only meant to teach the neighbor a little lesson, but a few days later, the old woman's kerosene stove had exploded, and everyone in the house had burned to death.

A rumor had circulated that she might have intentionally caused the fire. However, the police never managed to trace the crime to her. And yet…

"In the end, after losing a large sum of money to extortion over several years, the actress left a note and killed herself. In other words, she was not the one who penned this tale. It was her manager, the only person who knew the truth—or so the story goes."

"Huh? Wasn't *ubagabi*…?"

"Yes, it's probably the one mentioned in *The Illustrated Demon Horde's Night Parade*. An old woman who stole oil night after night, then manifested as a mysterious fire after her death."

"So the girl who wasn't quite human or demon was—"

"Mayuka. The man who told the actress about the inn was most likely Kazutora. He'd lure in people rumored to have done bad things, use Mayuka's eye to expose their sins, then blackmail them repeatedly."

After all, their victims were criminals who were afraid of the police. No doubt, more than a few gave in to the blackmail and paid out a fortune.

"In short, Mayuka didn't simply tolerate the fact that Kazutora and Ranko killed Kuniomi. She assisted with their crimes."

"But why would she do that?"

"It's conceivable that she was threatened… But that doesn't appear to have been the case."

That would mean she was also a Hell-bound sinner. But if that were true, something didn't make sense to Seiji.

"Um, then why does she still look human?"

"Hm?"

"I mean, if the man-eating inn story is true and Mayuka was in on it, shouldn't she look like a yokai, too? She hasn't changed once."

There was the *ungaikyou*, for example: the yokai version of the Mirror of Illumination. If Mayuka had abused the mirror's power long-term, it would have been an extremely appropriate shape for her, and yet...

"...I see. Yes, you're right," Shiroshi murmured. Putting a hand to his chin, he fell silent. In the depths of his eyes, Seiji could see his thoughts moving at a dizzying speed.

Um... I shouldn't get in his way.

Admonishing himself for his habit of interrupting, Seiji pulled his yokai art book closer. He meant to look up the *ungaikyou*'s page. He'd thought he might find a hint by reading the commentary, but before he got there, something unbelievable leaped out at him.

"Shiroshi! This! Look at this!"

The *jatai*.

In the picture, an obi that had been cast off in a bedroom was beginning to move and writhe like a snake. The artist had captured it in the act of lunging aggressively over a folding screen. And the longer Seiji looked at it...

"What I saw in the storehouse might not have been a *nureonna*. I think maybe it was this."

He'd probably felt that something wasn't right about the *nureonna* because he'd subconsciously remembered this picture. Buckling down and cramming the night before their trip had paid off.

Shiroshi's eyes were riveted to the drawing. When he spoke, he seemed to be talking to himself. "An obi that writhes like a serpent is a physical incarnation of the obsession of the woman who owns it. It belongs to the same archetype as *The Legend of Doujouji*, in which jealous love turns a living woman into a snake." His pale fingertip slowly traced the curves of the obi. "An individual is transformed into a wicked snake by a feeling that they yearn to consummate, even at the cost of their own humanity. This serpent hints at an inner Hell. In a word, it's much like a yaksha. However," he went on, "if what you saw was a *jatai*, my current line of reasoning doesn't hold together."

Shiroshi was right. His theory was based on the premise that Ranko's sin had been related to the *nureonna*. Seiji's revelation had destroyed its foundation.

"In that case, let us examine another possibility: Perhaps the *jatai* you saw was not Ranko."

"Huh?! B-but there was a funeral altar on the other side of the screen, and according to Mayuka, Ranko passed away this morning—"

"Yes. We put those things together and assumed that the body lying beyond the screen was Ranko's. However, we haven't actually seen it."

True. All Seiji's eye had picked up was the fact that there was a funeral altar behind the screen and that someone who'd taken the form of a *jatai* was there.

But if it wasn't Ranko...

"Then who does that body—?" Seiji had meant to finish with *belong to*, but he didn't get the chance.

"It can't be...," Shiroshi murmured. Then he fell silent. From his expression, he'd reached a conclusion that defied belief. "Oh, I see. In other words...this place is a Hell meant for me."

The remark was cryptic, and Seiji didn't get it. "Um, what do you...?" he started to say, bewildered.

Shiroshi only smiled at him. "Now then, Seiji, I have a favor to ask of you."

"...Wh-what is it?"

"Would you part ways with me here and go down the mountain first?"

"Huh? Just me? What about you?"

"Unfortunately, it appears I have a little more to do before I'll be able to leave." His voice was so cheerful that it seemed out of place.

As usual, Seiji didn't really understand what he meant. Actually, it felt as if Shiroshi was actively trying to keep him from catching on. "...No. No way."

"Pardon?" Shiroshi looked at him blankly. Then he smiled faintly, as if he'd figured it out. "I know you're frightened of running into snakes on a dark road by yourself, but—"

"No, not me. You."

"Me what?"

"I thought *you* might want to have somebody with you… I doubt you'll actually need anybody, but still."

Even so—if possible, he didn't want Shiroshi to go through something scary by himself. If he ended up in mortal danger the way he had on that island in Nagasaki, Seiji at least wanted to be there for him.

Granted, since Seiji was only Seiji, he might just end up getting in the way.

Still, if having me there could make even the slightest difference…

That was why he'd come with Shiroshi on this trip. If being with him was all Seiji could do, at the very least, he wanted to avoid leaving him on his own.

However…

Seiji knew that wasn't the real reason. He was more frightened than anyone. In fact, he was scared out of his mind. As scared as Mayuka had been of snakes and whistling.

He was terrified of losing his only friend again.

"You really are thoroughly you, Seiji." Shiroshi spoke slowly, as if he felt the words keenly. He leaned closer and looked right into Seiji's face. There was a wry edge to his smile. "At least in my case, you could have said you were staying with me as a favor, you know."

As Seiji sat there, stunned, Shiroshi caught his right hand, lifted it, and hooked his other little finger around Seiji's—a pinky swear.

"I promise we'll go home together. So wait for me, please."

Maybe…I'll just have to believe him.

After all, that soft smile was the same one Shiroshi always wore in the study.

"Okay, but you promised. Don't forget," Seiji told him. He changed out of the yukata and back into his clothes, returned his raggedy secondhand art book to his bag, then shouldered it. He took Shiroshi's bag, too, out of habit. Lately he didn't feel right if he was only carrying luggage for one.

"Ah, you've dropped something."

"Oh, thanks."

Shiroshi was holding out a pack of cigarettes; they'd been in the pocket of Seiji's down jacket. They must've fallen out as he was pulling it on.

"Do be careful."

"That's my line, Shiroshi."

After that, Seiji left the cottage.

He was scared he'd lose his way or run into a snake, but he made it through the covered walkway with unexpected ease, jumping the railing and cutting across the front courtyard just before he reached the main building.

The gate loomed eerily, towering over him. Passing through it, he made his way timidly down the stairs, using his smartphone to illuminate the ground at his feet. The mountain road that wound away from the foot of the stairs looked like an enormous snake.

What is this? The air feels different…

The wind was picking up. A sense of tension prickled his skin like the aura of an oncoming storm.

Something's…coming closer?

His rational brain told him it was just his imagination, but he was convinced it was lying through its teeth. His instincts were sounding an alarm, urging his heart to speed up. *Hurry, hurry, you have to get out of here right now.*

Because…

It's here.

He was being watched; he could feel it. It was as if a snake's unblinking eyes were fixed on him from the depths of the darkness.

Will it be a snake?

Or perhaps a villain or a demon?

"Agh!"

A gust of wind hit his back, strong enough that it almost sent him flying. Then it blew past him, blasting through the maples that flanked the stairs and rustling their red leaves urgently.

A moment later…

"…Huh?"

Seiji looked back at the stone steps; he was dumbfounded, his eyes wide.

He'd realized something unbelievable: the reason he'd felt strangely uneasy every time he saw the maples on this mountain.

I-it can't be…

There were no leaves on the ground.

Even after a gale like that, not a single leaf had parted from its branch. It was as if the sea of maples filling his vision were all exquisite fakes.

"The trees appear to be mountain maples, but their coloring is strange."

"The view is too uncanny to be magnificent. Frankly, I find it profoundly unsettling."

Shiroshi's voice seemed to echo in Seiji's ears.

Looking back…when they'd seen that mountain stream from the cottage, there hadn't been a single leaf on its surface. Ordinarily, the water should have been so thick with leaves that they looked like a red carpet.

There was something weird about this place. Something fatally wrong.

In addition, considering the things Shiroshi had said, he, too, had noticed how abnormal it was… And yet he'd stayed behind at the inn and sent Seiji home alone.

It was almost as if he'd made himself into a decoy to let Seiji get away.

"But that's ridiculous…," Seiji muttered, his voice cracking. At almost the same moment, his smartphone rang in his back pocket. Someone was calling him. Reaching the bottom of the stairs seemed to have put him back in the service area.

Maybe it's Beniko?

Feeling desperate, Seiji checked the screen, then made a startled noise.

It was Saori Toribeno.

Why is she calling me? …Oh, because Shiroshi's smartphone is out of range.

As a result, she'd tried Seiji, since he was technically Shiroshi's assistant. They'd exchanged contact information during the incident with Satsuki, and it had paid off at an unexpected time.

Sure enough, when he slid his finger across the screen and accepted the call…

"Oh, thank goodness. I've been trying to reach Mr. Saijou, and both calls and texts suddenly stopped going through. I thought something might

have happened." After hasty, minimal greetings, Saori spoke in a rush. She sounded relieved. *"I'm very sorry to call so late. I just had this awful feeling…"*

"It's fine, but um…is something wrong?"

There was a moment of hesitant silence. *"This might sound like a strange question, but the two of you haven't gone to the inn on that business card, have you?"*

As a matter of fact, I'm there right now, was the only possible answer Seiji could give. However, that would be admitting they'd stolen a march on her, so he didn't know what to say. As he was stalling and trying to figure out how to respond…

"The thing is, my chief editor has a drinking buddy from that village. I had them introduce me to someone who knows about the situation—a woman named Hatogaya."

"Huh? You mean the housekeeper from the journal?"

"Yes, that's the one. She used to work for the Asaka family, but she was fired when Kuniomi died. She still resents them for it."

…Apparently the vindictiveness she'd exhibited in the journal was still going strong.

"I spoke with her on the phone today, and she told me the inn went out of business quite a while back. It happened two months ago, after the step-mother died."

It was a full thirty seconds before Seiji found his voice again. "Um, wait, but…"

All he could think was, *That's crazy.*

It hadn't shut down. He'd been staying at the inn from the business card until just a few minutes ago. Not only that, but Ranko had died this morning; her body had been laid out in the storehouse.

"On top of that, Hatogaya said the address on that card was nonsense to begin with."

"Wh-what do you mean?"

"The Nine Echoes Lodge was apparently located on a modest hill surrounded

by a colony of azalea bushes. It was outside the village to the west, and the hill had a Jizo *shrine at its foot."*

"Th-then what was the address on the card?"

"She said it belonged to a temple in the mountains behind the station. It had originally had guesthouse facilities, but eventually there wasn't anyone left to take over, and no one lives there permanently anymore. It has no connection to Mayuka's family... Oh, come to think of it, she said there was a Jizo *shrine at the foot of that hill as well."*

Wasn't that...where Seiji was standing right this minute?

He tried to say, *It can't be,* but the words wouldn't come. The vague, uneasy feeling that had been smoldering deep inside him all this time gelled into various shapes and rose to the surface:

First, the fact that there hadn't been a reservations website, reviews, or any information at all about this place online.

Second, the way the inn had struck him as being "like a mountain temple" when he first saw it.

Third, the fact that he hadn't seen any of the things he would have expected to find at a typical inn, like a place to put valuables, a room phone, or even a sign with its name.

In short, the place where he and Shiroshi had been staying wasn't an inn called the Nine Echoes Lodge but an abandoned temple that should have been deserted.

"B-but why would Mayuka send a business card for...?"

"I don't know. And according to Hatogaya...Mayuka disappeared two weeks ago."

"...What?"

"Late on the forty-ninth day after Ranko's death, when her ashes had been laid to rest, Mayuka vanished. The head clerk Kazutora is missing as well."

Seiji was speechless.

It was way too strange. *He'd just seen both of them in person.*

"That can't be right!"

"Yes, considered normally, it wouldn't be possible. I argued with a man I

believe was Kazutora on the phone just a few days ago. They can tell me he's missing, but if my experience says otherwise…"

Writing it off as some kind of mistake would have made things nice and easy. However, when Saori had checked into it, she'd discovered that the police were indeed looking for the pair. In other words, they'd genuinely disappeared half a month ago. They'd simply evaporated one day, as if they'd been spirited away.

"Maybe they skipped town, then sneaked back in without being seen?"

"According to Hatogaya, Mayuka disappeared to avoid being questioned by the police. She said that although Ranko's death seemed to be due to illness, the truth was that Mayuka killed her."

…What?

"N-no, but she said Ranko had a congenital heart condition…"

"Yes, and the cause of death really was acute heart failure. She took medicine to lower her blood pressure every night. Apparently, she'd had a surgery two years ago that failed and made the issue worse."

"Then she *did* die of her illness after all, didn't she?"

"The thing is, Hatogaya said a vasopressor was discovered among Mayuka's belongings after she disappeared."

"A…vasopressor? What's…?"

"It's a medicine that raises blood pressure. If Ranko took that, it would have caused an arrhythmia and stopped her heart. Mayuka had assumed it would be treated as natural heart failure."

Seiji felt like he'd been hit in the head with a hammer.

If Mayuka had slipped some pills that would raise Ranko's blood pressure in with her regular medication, she could have poisoned her without attracting suspicion.

"Don't tell me Mayuka actually…"

Had it been revenge?

After all, as far as Mayuka was concerned, the woman had killed her father. Maybe she'd lived under the same roof with her until adulthood because she was frightened of becoming an orphan, but resentment had been building inside her the whole time.

Except…

"…Um, the thing is, I was just talking with Mayuka."

"What?"

Although he glossed over a few things in the middle, Seiji told Saori about meeting Mayuka and what had happened on their way to the cottage.

Saori fell silent for a bit, as if she was thinking hard. *"What did she look like?"*

"Well…fair-skinned and beautiful. She had amber eyes, and her face was almost like a waxwork doll's."

The second he said that, there was a small gasp on the other end of the line, and then…

"I don't think that was Mayuka."

"Huh?"

"Hatogaya said Mayuka had a purple birthmark on her left cheek. A twisting mark, like a snake. She said that was probably why her birth mother left her behind."

A line from the journal flashed through Seiji's mind.

That face of yours is a mark of the curse.

He'd just assumed she'd meant the extremely un-Japanese color of Mayuka's eyes, but she'd been making fun of a birthmark on her face.

But in that case…

"Then…who was the woman I met?" As Seiji spoke, his voice began to tremble. All of this was just too bizarre. If what Saori was saying was true, the "Mayuka Asaka" he and Shiroshi had spoken with was someone else entirely, an impostor. Someone was impersonating Mayuka.

But…who?

A terrible premonition made his spine crawl. His fingertips were growing cold, as if he had anemia, and yet his palms were sweating.

Unable to take it, he looked back. He could see the looming, silent gate in the depths of the red and black night.

What is going on at that inn?

He had an awful feeling about this. A devastating danger was creeping closer, slithering through the darkness like a snake. Closing in.

He didn't even have to ask who its target was.

At this point, the only guest stranded in that lodge in another world was Shiroshi.

That's it. I'm going back.

Ending the call almost without realizing he'd done it, Seiji started to run back up the stone steps, breaking his promise.

And then…

"Huh?"

A startled noise escaped him.

The wind had fallen still.

Words surfaced in his mind as clearly as if someone had whispered just behind his ear.

It's too late.

A moment later, the world was transformed into Hell.

The maples on either side of the stairs leading up to the gate, bright red against the night sky, and the deep red colony of trees that enfolded the inn and covered the mountainside behind it—in the space of a heartbeat, every one of them had turned to leaping, roaring flames.

The mountain itself seemed to have become a huge crimson serpent slowly raising its head.

It was a forest fire.

*

The family Ranko was born into had been spiritual mediums for generations.

Her great-aunt had served as her mother's midwife and had helped her through labor, and when she saw the newborn Ranko, she'd murmured, "This one hasn't been born properly. She looks like she's left half her soul in the other world. I doubt she'll live long."

As her great-aunt had predicted, Ranko had been born with a heart defect. However, she did survive…though perhaps it would have been better if she hadn't.

She was a girl close to monsters and close to the gods.

For some reason, Ranko had been born mute.

If left to her own devices, she was the sort of child who would spend all day gazing absently at the ceiling in the room where their Buddhist family altar was kept. She remembered a small dragon flying around and around the sooty ceiling, trailing thick black clouds behind it.

What Ranko saw was probably the realm of the dead, the world where she'd left half her soul. That world held countless spirits, goblins, and phantoms.

Ghosts, yokai, monsters, haunts, spirits, and apparitions—even after Ranko had developed a sense of self, the world she saw teemed with the inhuman and with beings that had once been human.

There were the arms of a woman with slit wrists wrapped around the neck of a door-to-door salesman like a scarf. The cat that often visited their garden was missing everything from the neck up. Had it been hit by a car and lost its head?

When she went to the living room for dinner, an imp with a long tongue was clinging to the soy sauce bottle, slurping up its contents. When night fell and she got into her futon, a woman no taller than her little finger was sitting by her pillow, strumming a shamisen. Her mother slept next to her; before long, a goldfish with human eyes flitted out from between her legs, and when its eyes met Ranko's, it wailed like an infant. It must have been something unborn that her mother hadn't kept.

Ranko's world was constantly revolving between this plane and the next, from reality to the fantastical, changing like a kaleidoscope. Or perhaps it was merely a daydream only the mad could see. Whenever Ranko saw these things, she'd come down with a fever, the worst of which would keep her sick in bed all through the night.

It was Ranko's parents who set her up as a "living god," turning her into a tool for their trade. When she took to her bed with a fever, villagers who'd heard the news would rush in with requests.

They'd ask for things like cleansing an illness, finding lost items, determining the success of a match, good omens for household luck, and so on.

Although Ranko was normally incapable of speech, while she was delirious with fever, she was able to relate "oracles." It was as if a god or demon had possessed her and was speaking through her. These oracles tended to be strangely accurate, and Ranko's family lived off the divination fees they collected from the villagers.

Ranko didn't remember ever attending school properly. She could hardly even read or write. Even when she did attend class, her classmates' parents would complain to the school.

Hurry and run that swindler out, they'd say.

The funny thing was that even the villagers who brought Ranko requests called her a "psychic fraud" behind her back. But whenever trouble befell them, they'd rush to grovel and beg for her help.

How utterly ridiculous.

However, after her first period—which arrived late—Ranko stopped coming down with fevers. She'd stopped seeing things.

Her panicked parents shut her in the bathroom in her underwear, forcing her to catch colds. She eventually came down with pneumonia, but it didn't change anything.

After that, Ranko was merely a nuisance and a useless mouth to feed. Aside from the men who sometimes gave her pocket money to sleep with them, she was shunned, treated as something others didn't even want to see.

That was when she met Mayuka.

A group of children were playing in front of the *Jizo* shrine at the foot of a hill of azaleas to the west of the village.

Kagome, kagome, the bird in the cage…

It was an old-fashioned outdoor game. Beneath the darkening indigo sky, the shadows of the children looked like imps, and nostalgia made Ranko stop. Just then, with a shout of laughter, the circle dragged in a small girl who'd been passing by.

Kagome, kagome, the bird in the cage…

Pushed and jostled from all directions, the girl crouched down in the center of the ring. Then the older boy directly behind her scooped up a double handful of sand and poured it over her head.

"The monster's gonna cry! Ruuuuuun!"

The children scattered in all directions. A few of them threw small rocks. The only one left was the girl they'd called a monster.

Is she really a monster?

Curious, Ranko crouched down in front of her.

The girl's sandy head snapped up, as if she were a frightened young animal. Frankly, Ranko hadn't been looking forward to dealing with a crying child, but there were no tears on the girl's cheeks.

My, Ranko thought, *she looks familiar.* The second the thought occurred to her, she realized why: She looked like Ranko's own reflection, seen in a mirror when she was very young—a face blank with resignation.

When she gestured to show that she couldn't speak, the girl nodded. She was clever; apparently, she'd understood.

But why would they call her a monster?

She was quite obviously human. As Ranko was puzzling over this, the girl—Mayuka—pointed at herself. In addition to surprise and bewilderment, her face held a twisted, serpentine birthmark.

"It's because I'm ugly."

Huh? Ranko tilted her head.

It wasn't as if she had horns or a third eye. Her features were human. There were only tiny differences between the girl and herself.

"That, and I see bad people as monsters."

Oh, I see. It all made sense to Ranko now. *So she's like me?*

Humans live in groups, and they're built to loathe those who aren't like them. Ranko had been neglected, detested, feared, and dreaded. As far as others were concerned, she was a snake in human form.

She'd lived alone on the border between this world and the world of spirits, a monster that only barely managed to pass as human.

This girl is like me, then? She might be the only one in the world who is. This girl alone.

Gently taking Mayuka's hands, Ranko kissed the birthmark that crawled over her left cheek. When she drew back again, Mayuka blinked at her, dazed. In that moment, her eyes seemed to match her age.

The change struck Ranko as funny, and she laughed, although she knew she shouldn't.

Finally realizing she was covered in sand, Mayuka hastily brushed it off, and this time, Ranko started sneezing and couldn't stop. Maybe some of the dust had gotten into her nose. At that, Mayuka burst out laughing. Those smiles, which looked almost tearful, were the first ones they shared.

Before they knew it, they were spending most of their days together, and then Ranko received an unexpected marriage proposal.

Kuniomi Asaka was a man of around forty who was listed as Mayuka's father in the official records. Although he was a big, square-jawed man, the old people of the village still called him "the landlord's young son."

He may have been a third son with nothing to inherit, but his revenue from real estate and land had given him enough of a fortune that he didn't have to work. As a result, he'd become an amateur scholar who spent all his time on research.

Although the marriage offer had come from a man old enough to be Ranko's father, who already had a child, her parents wanted the betrothal money. They readily gave their consent, and Ranko was sold, as if she were a dog or a cat.

Ranko was taken into Kuniomi's family as a wife, but in practice, she was always with Mayuka. The housekeeper, Hatogaya, took care of all the household chores and odd jobs. That meant Ranko's actual role was closer to "babysitter."

Hatogaya couldn't abide Ranko. She spent all day talking about her behind her back, and she didn't care who overheard. Her mistress was a sex maniac, a half-wit, a swindler. Ranko didn't need to be reminded that she wasn't very clever; she was well aware of that. Still, how could the woman have so much time on her hands?

Mayuka was an avid reader, and unlike Ranko, she was very smart. She stayed home from elementary school as much as she could, though, which meant the two of them were together all day.

Ranko couldn't speak, and similarly, Mayuka was extremely quiet. No matter how much adults tried to talk to her, she'd just shake her head or nod. When it was absolutely necessary, she'd respond with two or three words.

However, when Mayuka learned that Ranko had never properly attended school, she gradually began teaching her things. Times tables, kanji characters, division, multiplication... Ranko actually knew several of these things already, but Mayuka taught her carefully, one by one, breaking the subjects down like so many candy drops. In exchange, Ranko whistled for Mayuka whenever she asked.

In retrospect, those were curious times. They didn't make eye contact or exchange smiles. Just being together was enough to let them understand most things about each other.

Each was the only one the other would permit to stay at her side.

They weren't mother and child, or sisters, or even friends. It was simply that Mayuka was with Ranko, and Ranko was with Mayuka.

It felt as if they were allowed to be people only during the time they spent together.

Mayuka's voice calling her "Ranko" made Ranko human for the first time. It might have been lunacy to think that way, and yet...

As far as the two of them were concerned, those days were genuinely happy.

But then Kazutora Sawada came along.

He'd been hired because Hatogaya had hurt her back, and she pestered Kuniomi to employ a man. He was a sinister-looking drifter, and Mayuka said he appeared as a *dorotabou* to her. That made sense: Rumor had it that he'd begun as a land shark and had escaped to this area after doing some pretty vicious stuff.

Deceiving, plotting, threatening, beating—he smelled like the sort of person who knew and loved all these things. Just like Ranko's parents... And for petty thugs like him, Ranko was the perfect target.

Mayuka seemed to sense something. For a while, she stuck close to Ranko, never leaving her side. However, Ranko was alone at night, and the next thing she knew, Kazutora had approached her with a scheme to kill her husband.

He said he'd kill Mayuka if she refused. If she dared to tell anyone, he'd make sure the entire Asaka family saw the photos some men had once cajoled Ranko into letting them take of her. If that happened, she'd be forced to divorce Kuniomi, no matter how he defended her.

The Asakas had originally backed Hatogaya as Kuniomi's second wife. And in that case, the woman was bound to run Ranko off with a broom.

In the end, there was only one other path left for Ranko to choose.

That was why she was here now, on this May evening. Mayuka had caught the flu out of season and was sick in bed, and Ranko stood by her pillow, silently saying good-bye.

Perhaps "her final farewell" was a better way to put it. She was planning to throw herself in front of the morning's first train.

Even if she fled with nothing but the clothes on her back, she'd never have a decent life. She could escape from the birdcage, but unless she knew how to fly, she'd just fall and be eaten by animals.

She was worried about Mayuka, but if the girl had Kuniomi, she'd probably be fine.

She'd heard rumors that, as a child, Kuniomi had been bullied by his parents and siblings for his stammer, and that was why he'd begun to study martial arts. Other people still scared him, but he saw his former self in Mayuka. That must have been why he'd resolved to be her father. Mayuka was also the only reason he'd taken Ranko as his wife.

In the end, the two of them resembled each other, even if they weren't related by blood.

Please let them live, Ranko prayed.

She knelt by Mayuka's pillow, gently reaching out toward her cheek. She knew it would be warm if she touched it. Even if she'd never be able to touch it again, that fact made her happier than anything.

I'm sorry.

All her words stuck in her throat; those were the only two that finally escaped her. Since Ranko was mute, she couldn't say even that much aloud. Having wordlessly completed her farewells, she was about to rise to her feet, when…

Don't go.

Mayuka's lips trembled. She was murmuring deliriously. Her eyelids, damp with sweat from her fever, were still closed.

You're all I need, Ranko.

So please don't cry.

It wasn't until a large tear dripped off Ranko's chin that she realized she was crying. She knew that a tear had fallen on Mayuka's sleeping cheek and drawn those words from her.

Once she'd noticed, there was no going back. She couldn't deceive herself anymore.

I want to be with her.

I want us to stay together.

I want to live.

She held the girl's small body close, and for some reason, she felt as if she were the one being hugged. She knew they were each just as warm as the other, and she didn't think anything could make her happier than that.

And now the child was being kind enough to stay here, in her arms.

This girl is like me. She's alone. I've finally found something that's mine, and it's her.

She whistled very, very softly, careful not to wake the girl.

Since she couldn't speak, whistling had been how she'd cried. When she was kicked out in midwinter in nothing but her underwear, and she had to use her meager allowance to purchase shelter from single men, she'd whistled to take her mind off her situation.

Mayuka had been the only one who'd listened.

People said the sound of whistling at night was a dreadful thing, but Ranko was whistling a lullaby, and she wouldn't stop. Not even if dawn broke and nothing had changed, and the morning found her guilty of killing her husband.

Snakes and villains and demons.
If whistling at night summons you, then hasten to me.
If you wish to bite, then bite.
If you wish to steal, then steal.
If you wish to devour, then devour.
Even if my body is reduced to bones and my soul falls into Hell, I'm sure I'll
smile and say…

…this child alone is mine.

✱

The room was a gloom-filled box.

The moonlight that filtered in through the latticed window was faint, and the drifting incense smoke was nebulous. The walls on either side seemed to be lined with books, and it looked as if there was a folding screen directly in front of him.

He was in the storehouse.

"Hm. I was told we'd be admiring the moon over sake, but…" The boy smiled wryly.

Behind him, there was movement in the shadows.

A figure stepped into the moonlight. It belonged to a woman with amber eyes and a pale, strikingly beautiful face. She tilted her head. "Yes. All night long, if you'd like. I thought sleeping by yourself might be lonely."

"…That's hardly the sort of thing to say to a child."

"I'm saying it *because* you are a child." She gave him a graceful smile.

"My." The boy's eyes widened in astonishment. "Did I look too young to sleep alone?"

"I'll put you to sleep, if you wish. Perhaps you miss your deceased mother."

"No, thank you. First of all, it would surely be a repeat of *Ryutandan*," the boy shot back.

The woman's eyes narrowed until they resembled sharp blades. "Oh, you'd noticed?"

"When it's this blatant, one could hardly miss it. Although perhaps I should have picked up on it when I heard the inn's name." The boy gave a self-deprecating shrug. "'Crimson the way ahead, crimson the path already trod'—that line in the journal was a pastiche of one from Kyoka Izumi's *Ryutandan*. Oddly enough, the tale is a fantasy about a boy who's spirited away and encounters an enchantress in another world. It's set in a place called 'Nine Echoes' and shares its name with this lodge." As he spoke, the boy knelt in front of the screen, with its picture of crashing waves. His white kimono gleamed brightly in the shadows; against it, the pale gray of his Shingen bag looked like a drop of ink.

"'Azaleas the way ahead, azaleas the path already trod'—the original line refers to a hill of azaleas. In other words, the 'crimson' in the journal was meant to indicate azaleas, not red leaves. With every new season of snakes, the whole area is dyed red: That wasn't late autumn, when pit vipers appear, but the end of spring, when snakes emerge from hibernation. May is when torch azaleas are at their peak. In short, the lodge known as Nine Echoes should by rights be located in a colony of azaleas. At the very least, this isn't it. In other words...," the boy continued. "This entire place is a counterfeit. I imagine it was a trap, and Mayuka's journal and business card were the bait to lure us in. Am I wrong?" His gaze seemed to bore into the woman.

She gave an elegant shrug. "No. I borrowed an abandoned temple for a short while and cast a barrier around it. Where do you suppose the boundary was?"

"In all likelihood, the snake bridge before the stone steps. That marked the edge of another world. No doubt, the barrier covers the mountain itself. In other words, the moment we stepped over that snake, we were spirited away. That's why our cell phones lost service. Now we've been cornered, unable to summon any help from the outside world. In short, we're in a desperate predicament."

"You're quite perceptive. That's a great help. Parenthetically, you've been rendered unable to summon a single one of your father's yokai, let alone request aid from the Enma Ministry. The spell I cast on you ensures it."

A red leaf appeared at her fingertips.

She twirled it, toying with it, then pressed it softly to her lips. It was a familiar gesture—the boy himself had done it just after arriving at the inn.

Then the leaf warped, turning into a small crimson snake. Starting from the tip of its tail, it dissolved into smoke and vanished.

I see. So the red leaf that fell onto my breast was a sealing spell?

"I suppose I should say, 'You've tricked me,' but… Why don't we put an end to this farce, Ibara?"

"My." The woman's eyes widened.

Then she put a hand to her glossy black hairline and pulled off her wig, revealing hair of such a pale blond that it seemed white at first glance.

A white-haired revenant.

At the sight of amber eyes watching him through longish bangs, the boy felt an abrupt sense of déjà vu. Those, at least, were the same. They matched the eyes of the boy's fated rival, Odoro Rindou, who claimed his twin had died.

Yes, this was Ibara Rindou.

He appeared to be in his midtwenties, but his delicate build and pale skin made him seem more fragile than the boy. He looked as though, if he were struck, even his bones would shatter like waxwork, promptly reducing him to a corpse. However, the strangeness and chaos in his eyes undermined that first impression.

He was a bewitching flower whose fatal aura grew ever clearer as the night grew later and the darkness deeper.

"I had heard you were twins, but you don't really resemble each other."

"Mm, no. The thought that I might have looked like *him* isn't the least bit funny."

The pair wore opposing colors.

White.

Black.

One seemed to be dressed for his own burial. The other wore what appeared to be mourning clothes.

The dead and the mourner.

"I see," said Ibara. "From your expression, it looks as if you knew all along."

The voice that issued from his thin lips had changed completely. It was a whisper so faint that it was barely there, yet it reached Shiroshi's ears with an odd clarity. It was the voice of someone used to being obeyed.

"Yes, for about three months now."

"Since the incident on that island in Nagasaki, you mean?"

"Because a certain someone resurrected my youngest elder brother, it became necessary for us to have the Enma Ministry inspect the registry of the dead. When they did so, a certain question arose. With the exception of Odoro, the sixth-born, all of Shinno Akugorou's sons have died. However, there were signs that one of the records had been altered—yours."

"And so you thought I'd come back to life?"

"Come back? There was no need for that. In all probability, *you never died.*"

According to the records, he'd committed suicide. At the end of an extremely bitter fight over the succession, he'd killed himself in front of his twin.

However, his corpse had never been found.

"This resulted in a private investigation. At present, suspicion is focused on Shinno Akugorou. They suspect he hid you, his true heir, by making it appear that you had died, then positioned your younger twin as the heir. While Odoro competed with me out in the open, you, at your father's bidding, would attempt to do away with me covertly, from the shadows. That seemed the most natural way to interpret the situation."

In fact, the boy had supported that theory himself.

…Right up until he faced this man in person.

"However, I really can't see you as a filial son who'd submit to being his father's puppet."

A dry sound rang out.

In a theatrical gesture, the young man had clapped his hands.

"I see, yes. You do seem too much for my brother to handle."

"Well, on principle, I only fight opponents I know I can defeat."

The boy's words made the young man's smile deepen. "What a coincidence. I'm the same way."

The expression had a mocking edge to it.

He clapped his hands again sharply.

The screen instantly vanished, exposing a coffin.

The corpse that lay inside it looked like a Japanese doll put away in a box. It belonged to a young woman dressed in a white burial kimono. Her glossy black hair was cut straight across at her shoulders, and a bluish mark like a snake twisted over her left cheek. Her face was so peaceful that she might have been asleep…though her hands clutched the ends of a thin red obi she'd wrapped around her neck like a cord.

She'd strangled herself.

"…This is Mayuka Asaka? So she committed suicide…," the boy said, staring at the coffin.

The young man responded with a casual nod. "That's right. Having heard the rumors of the man-eating inn, I called on her, and that very night, though I hadn't asked, she confided her life story to me. Apparently, it was the forty-ninth night since her stepmother's death, and they'd laid her ashes to rest that day. She died without waiting for the dawn—half a month ago."

"What brought you here? Why now?"

"I thought it would make for a perfect riddle to lure you in. No doubt, it's a habit for those who run proxy services for Hell: Once you hear of a crime for which there has been no judgment, you feel compelled to uncover the truth. Just like an animal who stumbles into a trap while following the scent of its prey."

The young man shrugged casually. "Since we have the opportunity, why don't we check your final answer? That young woman's sin was the murder of her stepmother. She poisoned her by switching her blood pressure medication, making her death appear to be the result of her illness... And yet the sin your pet dog saw appeared as a *jatai*. How do you explain that?"

The boy lowered his eyelids. Keeping his eyes closed, examining each of his words carefully, he finally spoke in a subdued voice. "Since antiquity, the story of *jatai* and other tales of women becoming snakes have had one point in common. It's particularly conspicuous in *The Legend of Doujouji*. A woman pursues a man who runs from her, until at last she transforms into a snake. She burns her beloved to death; then, feeling as if life without him would be pointless, she throws herself from a bridge, *thus dying alongside him*. In short, the tales of women who've become snakes are always tales of murder-suicide."

His voice was as dispassionate and toneless as rain.

"Feelings a person wants to bring to fruition even at the cost of their own humanity turn people into snakes. However, once transformed, they can never change back. What such women have in common is a destructive obsession, the antitheses of self-preservation. This was true of Mayuka as well."

His eyes were on a serpent sleeping in the coffin. Like a deep crimson snake, the obi was wound around the girl's throat. In his book, Toriyama Sekien had drawn the *jatai* as an obi taking the form of a snake yokai lunging over a bedchamber screen to attack someone.

Perhaps its target had been the owner of the obi herself.

"When Mayuka killed Ranko," said the boy, "she'd already planned for it to end this way. Once her stepmother's ashes were interred on the forty-ninth day, she meant to follow her in death. In short, her sin was never 'murder'; it was murder-suicide. That may be why she took the form of a *jatai*."

In that case, this ending was probably not the result of hatred or anger, but of...

"Was she motivated by her love for Ranko?" asked the boy.

"*Obsession* is probably a better term. Ranko had grown conspicuously weaker over the past few years, and she'd realized that her death was near. What concerned her was Mayuka. She'd wanted to get her away from

Kazutora somehow, and the two of them had been planning to escape together. However…" The smile on the young man's lips deepened. "It was Mayuka who had suggested blackmail to the man in the first place. Ranko never knew. Until the very end, she was convinced that the girl was a victim who'd been dragged into their crimes. Ranko was a kind soul, and the more crimes they committed, the harder it was for her to escape from Mayuka, her accomplice. That was why Mayuka kept doing it. It was as if she were trapping a songbird in a cage."

Unbidden, a line from a children's song surfaced in the boy's mind.

Kagome, kagome, the bird in the cage…

That cage woven of sins had once held two birds. When one tried to escape, the other had killed it.

"Why…?" the boy moaned. His eyes looked as if he were fighting the pain of some invisible wound. "Ranko was trying to escape with her. They could have spent what little life she had left together."

And yet…

"Because only Mayuka was born ugly," the young man told him, as if it were only natural.

One's appearance at birth was like a congenital illness. Mayuka's face had, like a snake, provoked disgust since she was born. She didn't think she'd be able to live anywhere else.

And, with one exception, she'd thought no one could ever love her.

"Ranko was beautiful, Mayuka's polar opposite. Although she wasn't aware of it herself, it was her beauty that had made her a victim of others' lusts and caused the villagers to dread her. She was like the enchantresses in Kyoka Izumi's *Ryutandan* and *The Saint of Mount Koya*. People swarmed around her like moths to a flame. Mayuka knew that, if Ranko only escaped the birdcage, someone who genuinely loved her would appear before too long."

She didn't want to lose her. Didn't want to part with her.

This woman alone is mine—had that emotion been what transformed her into a snake?

"There's a similar snake inside you, isn't there?"

"…I don't know what you're talking about," the boy said coldly.

The young man gave a significant smile. "When I heard you'd begun keeping a human, I thought it was a clever move. The Enma Ministry's agreement doesn't cover those. A human you'd domesticated would be able to kill as many of your mortal enemies as you wished. I assumed you'd begun to train yours accordingly—but from the look of things, he's just a child's toy."

Ibara's lowered eyes held a kindness that was almost benevolence. It was the sort of look one of Hell's tormenting demons might occasionally show a child who'd died after being abandoned by their parents.

"You're frightened of others fleeing from you. You couldn't handle being betrayed, so in the end, all you've been able to keep with you are a goldfish in a bowl and a pet dog you've collared and chained. It's enough to make one weep."

"Silence, you wretch."

The boy's voice was low and flat, but his teeth were clenched, and the anger stealing into his expression was more intense than anything he'd ever shown—it was murderous.

"Well, well. It looks like I was right." The young man's voice was light-hearted and mocking.

Then he slowly raised his hands and clapped for a third time.

"Come."

The next moment, the boy's nose caught the smell of an animal.

A figure leaped down from the rafters and landed heavily on the tatami.

It was a middle-aged man whose face was wrapped in bandages. Through the small gaps between them, eyes peered out at the boy, glaring, as the man exhaled foul-smelling breath.

It was Kazutora Sawada.

"I thought I would show you how turning men into beasts is usually done," the young man whispered. He reached out, and the man's bandages unraveled and fell away.

The face they revealed was so ugly, it was hardly human. Or rather, at this point, it was less a face than a ruined mass of blackish scabs.

Behind the man's neck, near the hollow at its nape, a shadow moved.

There was a hole the size of the tip of his little finger there. Inside it, something squirmed, and then a small, deep red snake emerged. Slithering out of the cavity, it slowly tore off a scab on the man's face, then began to lap the blood and pus that welled up.

"*Ghk*, ah, ungh…"

The man groaned. It was doubtful that he was even sane anymore.

"That's from Kyokutei Bakin's *Tale of Eternity Rewarding Virtue*, isn't it?" said the boy. "As retribution for a man's misdeeds, a little snake makes its den in the back of his head, eventually eating all the scabs and flesh from his face and killing him—the story of a brutal villain who is devoured by his inner serpent, as it were."

Could you call this a fitting end for a scoundrel? Even if one couldn't pity him, it was simply cruel.

"That's right. As that snake's master, only I can stop it. This man seems to have eaten a living snake in an attempt to break the curse, but that could never work. As a result, he'll do anything I say. That's how he's been trained." A hand as white as a specter's grabbed the back of the man's head. Then Ibara peered into his eyes, just as a hunter would do to his prey. "This is what it means for an *oni* to keep a human. If you entrust so much as a corner of your heart to one, you're no longer an *oni*. You're just a lonely child. It's sickeningly pathetic."

Reaching into his kimono, the young man drew out a dagger. Smiling, he unsheathed it, then dangled it in front of the man's nose, as if he were offering meat to a dog. The man's trembling hand reached for the hilt— then he grabbed the blade with such force that it seemed as if it might break.

"Now what will you do?" the young man asked, turning back.

The boy was still kneeling calmly. Quietly, he shook his head; there was something like nobility in his expression. "I won't cry and beg for mercy. Nor will I make one last futile attempt to flee. I may not look it, but I do have my pride."

"…I see. That's a relief," the young man said, although he looked as if he actually found it rather boring. "In that case, let's send you to Hell."

There was a low, bestial growl. The man's darkly gleaming eyes peered out of his scab-covered face and fixed on the boy. Then, abruptly, the jagged surface of the man's face went slack. His lips seemed to split, curving, and a string of saliva dribbled from the corner of his mouth.

He'd sneered.

"There. Go." Ibara's pale finger pointed.

At the signal, the man's pupils constricted to tiny points.

They were the eyes of a snake targeting its prey.

And then—

"Ghaaaaaaaaaaaaah!"

—he unleashed a hoarse scream.

The boy had taken a small glass bottle from his Shingen bag and dashed its contents into the man's face. The smell of scorching flesh mixed with the stink of pus and blood.

It was concentrated acid.

While it couldn't melt bone, it was more than enough to cause blindness. He'd secretly brought it along for self-defense.

Leaping to his feet, the boy bolted like a deer, making straight for the open door.

He'd run.

"Unbelievable. Fleeing's his first and only option, hm? He's even less principled than I thought," Ibara whispered to himself. No one responded. Instead, broken screams welled from the throat of the man writhing in agony on the tatami, covering his face.

As Ibara watched, the screams died away, replaced by rough breathing. Then one glaring eye peeked out from between the man's burned, blistered fingers.

He could see.

He'd reflexively clapped a hand over his face, and that side was unburned.

"…Ah. First his dog ran, and now his goldfish? They lose as poorly as their master," the young man murmured.

By then, he was alone in the storehouse.

Autumn nights were long.

As long as a nightmare from which one cannot wake.

A small figure ran down the endless connecting walkway.

It never turned to look. It never stopped.

However, left with no way to protect itself, it was like a child pursued by a wild animal.

The man's hand grabbed its shoulder with brutal force.

The figure staggered, and as it began to turn back...

Was it fear? Dread? There was no knowing what emotion those eyes held.

Just as he'd done to the live snake, the man's leering mouth ripped out its pale throat.

*

Seiji felt as if he'd seen a huge crimson serpent leap into the night sky.

The fire that had now spread as far as he could see had probably given him that illusion. Like a magic trick, the tens of thousands of red maples covering the mountain's flank had become raging flames.

It had all happened before he could even blink.

He sucked in air in a whistling gasp, and burning pain ran through his throat. It was hot. Seiji couldn't even register the danger he was in, though.

Hellfire had swallowed everything around him. The gate that towered at the top of the stairs creaked, shooting sparks high into the air, threatening to crash down at any moment.

Flames had probably engulfed the inn beyond, too—like a great serpent coiling around it, crimson scales writhing.

Once it caught you, that would be the end. It would swallow you alive.

"...No."

Seiji's mind went blank, as if burned clean.

Nothing he saw felt real. The sounds seemed distant, as if he'd covered his ears. The wind that buffeted his cheeks was hot, and the sparks hurt his skin, but even the heat and pain seemed like a lie.

Moving almost involuntarily, Seiji took a shaky step forward, starting up the stairs.

Just then…

"Huh?"

…an unsteady figure emerged from the flames. It staggered, then toppled forward, beginning to fall headlong down the steps. Impulsively reaching out to catch it, Seiji realized the figure was dressed in a kimono.

No, not that one. It was red—this was Beniko.

"Beniko! Why?!"

Managing to catch her just in time, he dropped to his knees. He put an arm around her shoulders, helping her sit up. Then he saw something unbelievable on her cheek, which was as white as a Noh mask.

A single drop of water trickled from her black eye.

A tear.

Her trembling lips parted, and when she spoke, it was as if she were declaring the end of a dream.

"Master Shiroshi is dead."

MYSTERY 2
HIMAMUSHI NYUUDOU,
OR SUNEKOSURI

Three days.

It had been three days since Shiroshi had vanished in that inferno in the mountains of Okuhida. According to Takamura, who was leading the search, they still hadn't found any clues.

"It isn't just us. The police and fire brigade have cordoned off the area and are continuing their search, but they've had no results to speak of."

"…I see."

Takamura seemed tired, and Seiji couldn't look straight at him. He looked down instead.

As usual, they were in the study. The Queen Anne chair where Shiroshi always sat was unsettlingly empty.

"My, what's the matter?"

Seiji could visualize Shiroshi tilting his head, puzzled, but the sight existed only in his memories now. Even that seemed like it might blur and fade, and a permanent chill settled into Seiji's spine.

Even though it's only been three days…

Or had it been three days "already"?

"Some of the dignitaries seem to feel there's no hope of Master Shiroshi's survival. According to them, we should consider him dead and hasten to make our next move. And since the criminal may have carried him off, I'm not certain we can afford to spend more time searching the site."

"Th-that's true, but, I mean…"

In the end, it wasn't even clear who had been behind this incident.

On the heels of the affair in Kyushu, someone had used Mayuka's journal to lure Shiroshi and Seiji to that abandoned temple deep in the mountains. If the culprit had known that Shiroshi ran a proxy service for Hell, and if the mystery surrounding Kuniomi's murder had been part of a trap to keep him there, they'd been astoundingly thorough.

On top of that, a barrier so large that it defied belief had apparently been cast over the entire site. Because of that, the flames hadn't spread to the outside world, and the fire had been extinguished with unprecedented speed, but…

"Come to think of it, didn't they say they'd recovered bodies from the ruins?"

"Yes, the burned corpses of a man and a woman. From their teeth, they are presumed to be a pair of villagers who had been missing for half a month."

Kazutora and Mayuka. In the end, both had died without revealing anything about the incident sixteen years ago.

"Did whoever set the trap for us kill them, too?" asked Seiji.

"The police believe it was a murder-suicide. From the state of the bodies, they think the man probably strangled the woman with something like an obi first, then poured gasoline over his head and set himself on fire… However, no one knows for certain. Beniko will have been the only witness, and she is as you've seen." His tone was solicitous.

Seiji squeezed his hands into tight fists on his knees.

"Master Shiroshi is dead."

Beniko's words still lingered in his ears.

At the time, she said, she'd been hiding nearby, on Shiroshi's orders. In other words, she'd been keeping an eye on the two of them like a ninja, the way she had during the Shidou family incident. That meant she'd probably witnessed everything that had happened in the inn after Seiji had headed down the mountain.

However…

"…I can't remember."

Even after Takamura had appeared out of the ether as usual and taken her and Seiji into custody, Beniko had kept mechanically repeating those words.

Apparently, she'd had a shock that had temporarily impaired her memory. If *something that bad* had happened to Shiroshi...

Feeling a surge of nausea, Seiji put a hand over his mouth.

Right up until this happened, he genuinely hadn't understood that Shiroshi could actually die.

"I promise we'll go home together. So wait for me, please."

He'd never considered the possibility that promise could end up becoming a lie.

He's alive.

He'll come home.

All Seiji wanted was to believe that, and yet...

The memory of Inokoshi dead in that moldy bathroom abruptly flashed through his mind, and he swallowed what reflexively welled up inside him.

I know.

When somebody died, that was it. There was nothing after that. Nothing, period.

Nothing at all.

"However, a parallel search for the mastermind is still being conducted. If there are any developments on that end, there may be something we can do."

"Are you leading that one as well, Takamura?"

"No, Great King Enma himself has taken command. Since Shinno Akugorou is suspected of having been involved, it's possible that the agreement with the Enma Ministry has been violated."

Ah. So as the judge, he needed to find out who was responsible for the violation.

The agreement made through the Enma Ministry specified that, until the contest to send sinners to Hell was decided, neither camp was allowed to harm the other. If this incident turned out to have been a plot by Shinno Akugorou's faction, it would be the clearest violation imaginable.

"He insists he knew nothing about it, but that may not be true. However, at present, we must consider him innocent until proven guilty."

"Um, then is it possible that Odoro was in on…?" Seiji hadn't even finished his sentence before he shook his head. *Nah. There's no way.*

It was completely unlike him.

Odoro Rindou was an arrogant jerk who still viewed Shiroshi with contempt for being only half-supernatural. As far as he was concerned, using foul play against an opponent that far beneath him would have been an everlasting embarrassment. Calling him "proud" sounded like a compliment, but broadly speaking, he was an idiot.

"We're having him stay at his agency just in case, but yes, the possibility that he was involved is extremely low."

"But then who…?"

Exactly. That put them right back where they'd started. In the first place, Seiji knew only bits and pieces about the situation. Takamura was keeping him up to date like this only out of kindness.

Although I'm sure he's worried about Shiroshi, too.

"Come to think of it, have you known Shiroshi long?" asked Seiji.

"Yes, I would say so. I made Master Shiroshi's acquaintance before he was old enough to remember me. After all, it was I who cast the charm to keep people away from his residences."

Whoa.

"As a result, I occasionally came by to make small talk and play sugoroku with him. When we first met, I thought, 'It can't possibly be all right for a child to be such a force'…and he hasn't changed much, really."

I bet not. Seiji nodded, smiling faintly.

The look in Takamura's eyes softened. "And so I believe he is alive. He is Master Shiroshi, after all."

He bowed respectfully, taking his leave, and vanished.

After that, Seiji was alone with that empty Queen Anne chair.

I guess I'll go back upstairs for now.

With a little sigh, he got up and quickly left the study, as if he were running away from it. The three of them had cheerfully taken tea in here only three days ago. At this point, that felt like a distant dream.

Just then, his eyes fell on the goldfish bowl in the bay window.

"...Huh?"

Something seemed off. Seiji stopped, perplexed.

Are the goldfish's pearl organs gone?

That couldn't be right. Ending its spawning season in just three days? Just how passive could you get?

It's not sick, is it? He ran a hasty search on his phone, and then...

"What?"

...he blinked. He'd stumbled onto some information that he found hard to believe.

It was a site that explained how to tell male and female goldfish apart. If the anal vent seemed to stick out slightly when the fish was viewed from the side, it was a female—which meant the goldfish he was looking at was a girl.

No, but only the males develop pearl organs, and I know it had those before.

Did goldfish undergo sex changes from out of nowhere? Did they turn male again if you dumped hot water on them? Was this a good old anime from the '90s?

As he was staring fixedly at that anal vent...

"So this is where you were."

When he turned around, Beniko was standing there.

She was wearing her familiar red-and-black Japanese maid outfit and carrying a small mountain of laundry. Her voice was a little hoarse, but at first glance, she looked the way she always did. Only...

"Whoa, wait, is it okay for you to be up?"

After all, she'd been rejecting all treatment and visitors and had refused to come out of her room. Seiji had hung bags with packaged rice porridge and jelly drinks from the convenience store on her doorknob to make himself feel better; frankly, he'd been beside himself with worry that something awful might happen to Beniko as well.

"I'm sorry to have worried you. However, I mustn't take to my bed when no one else has."

"Still, I mean, you shouldn't push yourself… Wait, isn't that my down jacket?"

"It was terribly soiled, so I thought I would send it out for cleaning."

"Yikes. Actually, yeah, that's a lot of soot stains and scorch marks."

Apparently, after seeing him go three days without noticing it was covered in ash, she'd snapped and collected it. At a glance, he didn't just appear pseudo-homeless; he looked like an arsonist fleeing the scene of the crime.

"Um, if you like, I can take it to the cleaners—"

"No, don't trouble yourself. More importantly, this was in the pocket." Beniko held out a familiar pack of cigarettes. Now that she mentioned it, for the past three days, the idea of smoking had completely slipped his mind.

He assumed she was going to confiscate them and give him dried squid again instead, but…

"I thought I would return them, if you'd like."

"Huh? It's okay if I smoke?"

"Yes, if it will make you feel better."

In her own way, Beniko was concerned about Seiji.

It made him feel self-conscious and also pathetic. Beniko's shock had kept her bedridden until just a few minutes ago; Seiji's anxiety couldn't even be a tenth of what hers was, and yet…

"I'll go outside."

He gave her a quick bow, then started for the entryway. Thinking he'd cool his head while he was at it, he stepped through the open door without taking a jacket.

The great sacred anise tree was right there. It was an evergreen whose leaves never turned, but now that it was autumn, it had produced star-shaped fruits that resembled anise pods.

The tree's other name meant "wicked fruit," and true to this, the pods were extremely poisonous. So much so that, while this was considered a sacred tree that purified evil, it was simultaneously dreaded as a symbol of death itself.

Hunching against the chill autumn wind, Seiji sat down on the approach to the front door. In what was almost an unconscious habit, he smacked the pack lightly, planning to take the cigarette that popped out, but...

"Huh?"

...none did. Something seemed to be stuck in the carton. When Seiji peeked inside, he spotted a twist of paper in among the tightly packed cigarettes.

What's this?

Pulling it out, he unfolded it. It was a scrap about the size of his palm, with a single line of writing across its center.

I'm alive, so please don't worry. Ask Beniko for your next instructions.

The handwriting was Shiroshi's.

"Huh?"

For a moment, Seiji was so startled that he stopped breathing. He caught himself looking around; naturally, Shiroshi was nowhere in sight.

He can't have sneaked back home so quietly, we didn't notice, right?

He hastily shook his head, canceling out the ridiculous idea. *No, come on, no way.* At the same time, he remembered something. Three days ago, when he'd last seen Shiroshi, he was pretty sure...

"Ah, you've dropped something."

"Oh, thanks."

During that exchange, Shiroshi had handed him this pack of cigarettes. He'd just assumed they'd fallen out of his pocket when he put on his jacket, but...

Maybe this note was already in there?

Thinking back, when Seiji had gotten lost and wandered into the storehouse, his down jacket had been in the cottage the whole time. If Shiroshi had taken the pack of cigarettes from his pocket and planted the note then...

Did he know things would end up like this all along?

And even with that knowledge, he'd been certain he could survive. Meaning...

"...He's alive?"

No, wait. Since Seiji had no idea how he'd escaped from that hell or where he was hiding now, blindly believing this was probably the height of foolishness.

Still, trusting Shiroshi was all he could do at this point.

"Beniko!"

When he burst into the study with a shout, Beniko turned, pressing a finger to her lips. "If that's made you feel better, I'm glad."

At that, Seiji was pretty sure he understood.

Beniko had read the note as well. Like Seiji, she was convinced that Shiroshi was alive—that must be what was going on. That was why she'd been able to get up, when she'd been practically dead to the world before.

But...

Um, if I'm not supposed to talk about it...does that mean someone's listening to us?

That was probably what her gesture had meant. That "someone" might be the mastermind behind this string of incidents.

Come to think of it, if Beniko had found the letter first, she could have simply told Seiji about it. The fact that she'd gone to the trouble of sending it to him in his pack of cigarettes meant that the situation had compelled her to.

"Um, Beniko, I have a favor to ask." Going to stand directly in front of her, Seiji drew a deep breath. "Tell me what I can do, please. Just a hint is fine. If there's even one thing..."

Unintentionally, an urgent note crept into his voice. For a moment, Beniko's black glass eyes wavered with unexpected intensity, then she quickly looked down. "Actually, Master Shiroshi asked me to relay a message to you if you returned from your journey alone."

"Wh-what is it?"

"Please visit Odoro's detective agency and stay there for as long as you can."

"...What?"

This must be what it felt like to get tricked by a fox spirit. He understood what she was saying. It was coherent Japanese, but...

"Huh? He wants me to go harass Odoro?"

"No. In fact, he would like you to be his assistant for a few days."

"Huh?!"

His voice cracked dramatically.

He would have been able to accept it more easily if she'd told him to go to Alaska and capture a grizzly. Not to mention that this mission was just about as dangerous.

"Wh-what on earth is the point?"

"I really couldn't say. However, he said you were the only one he could ask, Seiji."

...Maybe he should just pretend he hadn't heard this.

Frankly, unless he covered his ears and made a run for it right now, there was no guarantee he'd survive.

But... Seiji swallowed hard. Somewhere in there, his lips had dried out and stuck together, and he forced them apart.

"Um. Where is the Rindou Detective Agency?"

*

...And that was how Seiji had ended up here.

According to the map app on his phone, the building he was looking up at was his destination.

Is this really the place, though?

It was a terribly old three-story building. Dead vines crawled across its blackened stone exterior, as if trying to hide the cracks.

Although it had to be close to three in the afternoon, the sun was hidden behind an oppressive layer of clouds.

The imposing building, located in a sophisticated, first-class business district in the heart of Tokyo, had clearly escaped destruction during the war. Combined with the black rain clouds that hung overhead, it was like a scene straight out of a horror movie.

A haunted house... Well, yeah, it's definitely that.

After all, this was the headquarters of the Detective Who Summons Death. On top of that, he was actually the son and heir of Evil God Shinno

Akugorou. Faced with someone like that, the denizens of your average haunted house would probably flee without bothering to grab their shoes.

Seiji swallowed hard. He had the nerves of someone about to step into the cage of a ferocious animal. Just hanging back and looking up at the facade was giving him goose bumps and making his pulse race.

When he approached the main entrance, he found a set of glass double doors under an old-fashioned incandescent globe light. He couldn't see any figures on the other side. He also didn't see anything resembling an intercom. Granted, even if he had, he wouldn't have had any idea what to say.

"Please visit Odoro's detective agency and stay there for as long as you can."

No matter how he thought about it, that was insane. However, apparently it was the one thing he could do for Shiroshi, and if so…

I can't waste my time worrying about how it looks.

Cursing silently to himself, Seiji started to take that first step.

But just as he did…

Now then, Seiji, shall we go?

Seiji felt as if he'd heard that voice from half a step ahead, and out of nowhere, his heart constricted. However, no matter how much he blinked, he didn't see the back of a white kimono.

He was alone.

The depths of his nose stung, and he tipped his head back, looking up to distract himself from the sensation. A drop of rain fell on his cheek, as if the sky had spit on him.

Those clouds had finally begun to cut loose.

"E-excuse me."

When he hesitantly stepped through the door, he found himself in a narrow hallway. Going forward seemed to be his only option.

There was an old elevator at the end of the hall. It had a brass scissor gate that had been polished until it gleamed, and it was as much of an antique as the building's exterior.

… This thing still works, right?

He really hoped it wasn't designed to prank riders by having the cable snap and send them plummeting straight to Hell the moment they stepped inside.

Argh, I'll risk it. He leaped inside and pressed the "up" arrow. He heard the sound of gears meshing, and then the elevator ascended to the second floor, shaking and rattling ominously.

There was a languid *ding*, and then...

"Huh?"

The room he found himself in was much larger than he'd expected.

He'd just assumed he'd end up in an elevator hall, but this space was open from the first floor all the way to the third. Each floor seemed to be configured like a loft. Seiji was currently on the second one.

"Wh-what is this place?"

He felt as if he'd been bewitched somehow.

When he looked around curiously, he was startled to see that the entire right-hand wall—which was a full three stories tall—was monopolized by an enormous bookshelf.

The floor was made of lustrous black oak. Close to the elevator, there was a leather upholstered reception set. At the back, there was an area that looked like a study, its rear wall lined with document shelves. A razor-thin laptop sat on an antique executive desk. It looked just like the sort of private detective's office that showed up in foreign dramas.

"So this is really..."

...the Rindou Detective Agency?

Just then, Seiji heard a series of metallic *clangs*.

He flinched hard, turning toward the sound. There was an iron spiral staircase on his left, and someone was walking down it from the third floor.

Oh, crud!

Seiji bolted out of the elevator and hastily searched for a place to hide.

"Yes, as I said, even if it is a direct request from the Metropolitan Police Department, I'm refusing it this time," said a familiar-sounding voice. "A rather difficult individual has placed me under house arrest."

There was a muffled yell that seemed to come from the speaker of a cell phone. *"Huh?! Don't give me that bull. If we tossed you into a cage at the zoo, you'd pry the damn thing open with one hand; that's the sort of guy you are."*

"Well, I plan to consider it as a vacation and relax. Just three days ago, I was compelled to accompany you on an all-night stakeout."

"Don't you lie to me! You were in dreamland in three seconds flat, eye mask and all!"

Finally, Odoro appeared. He was in shirtsleeves; a suit jacket was draped over the arm that held his flip phone, which he'd put on speaker mode. With his other hand, he was dexterously tightening his tie.

From the fully audible conversation, he seemed to be talking with a detective from the Metropolitan Police.

No, hang on. Did this guy just get out of bed? It's three in the afternoon.

Seiji recoiled in shock, but he managed to swallow his silent criticism, and then…

"Excuse me. It appears I have a rat problem."

Odoro's footsteps stopped.

There was a *beep* as he ended the call.

"…Sorry to disturb you."

Reflexively pulling an about-face, Seiji tried to flee back into the elevator, but—

Bam. Dust danced in front of his nose.

Odoro's kick had stabbed into the wall, blocking Seiji's retreat. If his aim had been off by just a few centimeters, that foot would have shattered Seiji's skull.

…Isn't this greeting a little scarier than necessary?

Shuddering, Seiji stood there petrified, dripping with cold sweat.

"Now, then." Shutting his flip phone with a snap and putting it in his pocket, Odoro cracked his fingers audibly. "May I ask what brings you to my office?"

"Um… Uh, I was hoping you could let me stay here for a while."

"I see. Why?"

"I-if there's anything I can do, like odd jobs, or, um…" He couldn't bring himself to say, *Make me your assistant.*

"…Oh-ho?" Odoro's face was as expressionless as a Noh mask, but one of his eyebrows rose. Then he gave a contemptuous snort. "Searching for a new master already, hm? Changing camps before it's even clear whether your former owner is alive or dead. What a faithful hound you are. Or so I'd like to say, but…"

Abruptly, he reached out and grabbed Seiji by the throat. His bony fingers constricted around Seiji's windpipe like a collar, their fingernails biting into his skin. Slowly leaning in so that his face was close to Seiji's, he spoke in a bone-chilling voice.

"Who put you up to this?"

Seiji didn't know what he meant. Even if he had, he was in no state to answer.

"I really doubt you're clever enough to give up on your master. When it comes down to it, you leave everything in the hands of others. That means it's only natural to assume you're here on someone else's suggestion. Am I wrong?"

He'd called it in one. Seiji looked as if his throat had been packed with lead, and he couldn't suppress a groan at the pain of those fingernails—or rather, at the sharpness of Odoro's words stabbing into him.

After all, it was just as the man said.

During the three days since Shiroshi's disappearance, all Seiji had been able to do was wait. He still didn't really know what he should be doing.

However…

"Even so, I have to do this, no matter what." Seiji was being entirely genuine about that. In the end, there was only one reason: "Shiroshi believed what I saw, so I figure it's my job to believe what he thinks. That means right now, this is the only thing I can do…"

The words were almost a prayer.

When Odoro heard that, for some reason, he fell silent. He opened his mouth to say something but promptly shut it again. Then, abruptly, he *tsked*.

"…Indeed?" he said, almost whispering. His hand tightened around Seiji's throat, the nails digging in deep enough to draw blood. "Tell me this, then: If that half-breed's missing, exactly where and how did you learn what 'Shiroshi thinks'?"

Oh. Seiji's expression gave him away. *Not good.* He'd planted his foot solidly in his mouth.

"I thought it was strange all along. Would that devious schemer really behave and turn to ash for a mere forest fire? It seemed far more likely that he'd feigned his disappearance and was plotting something in the shadows. And you see, just as I was beginning to suspect that, you appeared."

…Who'd have thought he'd pick up on that possibility on his first try? In a way, maybe this guy was on the same wavelength as Shiroshi.

"All right. You will stay with me until you confess. Fortunately, I have nothing but time, and the lack of entertainment has left me in low spirits. Crushing one arm shouldn't soil the floor too badly."

Oh, crud. Saying he was going to get killed would have been a severe understatement. Seiji shuddered, sweating bullets. His gaze was wandering this way and that, when…

Odoro's cheek twitched.

Huh? Seiji cocked his head, and then his ears caught a low buzzing noise. It was the flip phone in Odoro's pocket. This exquisite timing— could it be…?

"My apologies for the interruption. I have an urgent notice regarding Master Seiji."

Just as he'd expected, it was Takamura. Wordlessly, Odoro shoved the phone right in front of Seiji's nose. It held a Line chat screen showing an ongoing call.

"After receiving a declaration from Master Shiroshi and conferring multiple times, we of the Enma Ministry have decided to officially acknowledge Master Seiji as a member of Sanmoto Gorouzaemon's faction. Therefore, please note that if you intentionally harm him, you will be considered in violation of the agreement and lose by default."

As an aside, apparently this decision had been an exception among exceptions.

"After all, modern pets are practically members of the family."

…Okay, tough it out. If I comment on that one, I lose.

"I'm also told that he's currently imposing on your agency. I will come to retrieve him tomorrow, so please look after him there for today."

A *vwoop* issued from the screen.

The stamp he'd sent showed a cartoony, bowing Shiba Inu carrying a bundle on its back, along with the words *Thank you for your hospitality.*

"…What do you suppose this is?" asked Odoro.

"Um, I'll ask him to read the room a little better when he uses stam—"

"That isn't what I meant."

"Of course it isn't!"

Finding himself hauled up by his shirtfront and sensing genuine murderous intent, Seiji's voice cracked.

Then the phone *vwoop*ed again.

"Parenthetically, as long as Master Seiji accompanies you, you may go out whenever you wish."

Apparently, outings were permitted if he had a guard. When Odoro put his flip phone away, he looked as if he'd aged a decade all at once. "In terms of compensation, that's quite…" He seemed to swallow the word *cheap*.

Just then, the room appeared to rock, as if an earthquake had struck.

"Huh?"

Seiji's knees gave out, dumping him on the floor.

Huh? What?

.He hastily tried to get up, but his legs were too weak to support him. He recognized these symptoms: He'd ended up like this in the past, when he'd gone three days without eating before payday at his part-time job and his blood sugar had dropped too low. Basically, he'd collapsed from hunger.

But it's not like I'm hungry or…

Just as he was starting to puzzle over it, a shocking realization hit him.

He couldn't remember eating once during the past three days. He'd made trips to the convenience store daily to get food for Beniko, but he'd completely forgotten about his own meals.

"Hm. When the useless mongrel act is taken this far, it's almost intimidating," Odoro said, stroking his chin. He looked genuinely impressed.

Leave me alone!

Seiji would have dearly loved to scream those words at him, but if the guy actually *did* leave him alone, he was pretty likely to die in a ditch.

Just then, the flip phone in Odoro's pocket vibrated, and Seiji heard a powerful *Tch!* It was Takamura again. Odoro disappeared downstairs, then returned with a brown paper bag.

"Lower your head and move one step back."

"Whoa, wait, what are you going to do?" Seiji growled, but Odoro hit him with a threatening look, so he grudgingly lowered his head and backed up.

And then—

"Ow!"

The bag fell from Odoro's hand, scoring a direct hit on the back of Seiji's head with a solid *clonk*.

"Beg pardon. I meant two steps," Odoro said calmly, with a deliberate shrug. He'd absolutely done that on purpose.

Dammit, go get your throat chewed on by a nue *again.*

Seiji glared at him resentfully. Then, realizing the paper bag held a can, he blinked in surprise. The label was written in English, but he managed to make out the words "sardines in oil."

Poison, huh? he thought, feeling like one of Tsuchiya's *Faithful Elephants.* He glared at the can for a little while.

"If I intended to kill you, I would just snap your neck." Odoro gave him a rather disgusted look from beneath half-lowered lids.

True, Seiji thought. Deciding to accept the handout gratefully, he picked up the can.

"…Why did that convince you?"

Ignoring Odoro's grumbling, Seiji tried to open the lid, but it was apparently the sort that needed a can opener.

"Um, can opener…?" he asked timidly.

The only response was a surge of murderous hostility.

Right.

Perhaps he could make like an otter and whack it open against something. He was looking around for a pointy object, when…

Hm?

He'd noticed that there was a leather upholstered chair by the window.

It was probably an antique. Its delicate cabriole legs were as slim as high heels; in contrast, the armrests had a royal dignity about them, and their leather upholstery was as lustrous as polished wood.

If Shiroshi had been here, he probably would have curled up there and read for hours.

Um, maybe if I pinned this under one of those legs, I could punch a hole in the top, Seiji thought, in an extremely ridiculous brainstorm.

"Don't touch it," Odoro snapped, shooting him a piercing glare. His voice was icy cold. Apparently, he was very attached to that chair.

However…

…Hm?

Odoro cast a quick glance at the piece of furniture, then averted his eyes, as if running from it. His expression was odd; there was sadness in it, or maybe irritation. It was as if he were fighting the pain of an old wound.

Just maybe…, Seiji thought.

Did that chair also hold memories of a former owner? Had it been someone's regular seat, like Shiroshi's Queen Anne chair?

Then, ever since that person went away, he's…

Had he been unable to touch it or even look at it properly, simply keeping it near him as a trace of someone who'd once been there, and as proof that they were gone?

There's something a little weird about that chair, though. Seiji tilted his head, puzzled.

He'd spotted something very unnatural. Normally, it wouldn't have seemed odd at all, but if this chair were as important to Odoro as it seemed to be…

"…Hm?"

Abruptly hearing the sound of machinery from the floor below, Seiji gulped. The elevator was in motion. Someone was on their way up.

Is it a client?

From the dubious look on Odoro's face, though, this was an unexpected guest.

There was a *ding* as the elevator reached their floor, and then…

"Hello? Excuse me… Oh my. I'm sorry for coming in without permission. I looked, but I didn't see a bell."

The visitor was an elderly woman of around seventy, carrying a folded raincoat over one arm. She wore a thick cardigan in a genteel way, and her thin white hair was pulled back in a small bun. She was pushing one of those combination chair-walkers. Her back was a little bent, but her plump cheeks had a healthy glow to them, and there was a Shiba Inu–like charm in her cute, round eyes and the crow's feet at their corners.

She folded the raincoat up and put it away in its pouch, then put that into the flower-patterned bag attached to her chair-walker. There were supermarket flyers, among other things, sticking out of the side pocket.

A pair of eyes couched in wrinkles looked curiously around the room, then registered Seiji on the floor. "Wh-what's the matter? Are you feeling sick?"

"No, um, I haven't eaten in three days, so…"

"Goodness, that's terrible!"

The second she heard Seiji's pathetic story, she began rummaging through her flowered bag, which was apparently insulated. Then she brought out a small container. "I'm afraid it's just my leftovers from lunch, but…"

When he opened the lid, it turned out to be inari sushi. Two lumps of moist, fried, sweet-smelling tofu sat there in small rounded mounds.

"Th-thank you very much!"

Seiji clapped his hands together in worship, then gratefully helped himself. As he chewed, the vinegared rice and the sweetness of fried tofu gradually soaked into his stomach. On an empty belly, nothing could have been tastier.

…Hm?

He blinked. He'd caught a faint, strange odor.

Was something rotting?

For just a moment, he thought he'd smelled rotten raw meat—or, no, had he?

Before he could trace the smell, it dispersed. While Seiji was still puzzling over it...

"By the way." Odoro, apparently tired of waiting, interrupted, as if he were stabbing the others with an icicle. "You've entered someone else's office without permission and begun feeding a stray, but who exactly are you? Where have you come from?"

At first glance, his face was as expressionless as a mask, but on closer inspection, a twitching vein stood out on his temple. He was very close to completely losing it.

Seiji shuddered hard, but the elderly woman gave a surprisingly casual bow. "Oh, I'm sorry. I haven't introduced myself yet. My name is Suzu Torikai. I was told I could consult with a detective if I came here."

"I don't know who told you that, but this agency operates exclusively on a system of introduction. If you don't have an appointment, I'm afraid I can't meet with—"

"Oh, that's right. He gave me your card."

The card Suzu produced was very familiar, with *Rindou Detective Agency* in gold letters on a black background. However, the name printed beneath those words was...

"...Ibara?" Odoro's stunned murmur seemed almost involuntary.

Ibara Rindou.

If Seiji recalled, that was Odoro's twin brother, the second detective who'd started this agency with him.

Except...I thought he was dead.

According to what Seiji had heard, there had been a ferocious succession battle, and Odoro was the only one of his thirteen brothers who'd survived.

On top of that, it had happened more than five years ago, before the contest to send sinners to Hell began.

"Who gave this to you? How many years ago was it?" Odoro's voice was unnaturally flat. His expression had gone from astonished to completely blank.

"When was it? Yesterday?" the woman said. "...It does feel as if it may have been several years ago, though. I remember it was a young man who gave it to me, but I can't recall who he was... I'm sorry." Suzu shrank into herself slightly, looking apologetic. "Maybe it's my age. I seem to know less and less these days."

Hm. Apparently, she was extremely forgetful.

"...I see," Odoro murmured. He put a hand to his chin and thought for a while but didn't seem to get anywhere. "To begin with, why don't you tell me the reason for your visit? Please, have a seat." He gestured toward the reception set.

After seating herself with some effort on one of the clearly expensive leather sofas, Suzu looked around curiously. "This is a very nice office. Did you decorate it yourself?"

"My elder brother was very particular about that sort of thing. I didn't even touch the blueprints... Would you care for some coffee?" Responding with unexpected frankness, Odoro crossed to the study area. The space was equipped with a cupboard, and a hand-cranked coffee mill and jars of coffee beans sat on the counter.

Before long, Odoro handed her a cup brewed from freshly ground beans, with a few sugar cubes on the side.

"My, how kind of you." Accepting the coffee, Suzu blew on it, then took a sip and savored it. "Oh, that's delicious. You've given me an extra day of life."

It seemed as if she might mean that literally.

...Naturally, Seiji hadn't been offered so much as a glass of water. Or a chair, even.

Carrying a cup for himself, Odoro sat down on the opposite sofa.

"Let's see. Where should I begin...?" Behind the steam rising from her cup, Suzu started to speak, hesitated, then tried again. "It's the dog, you see. She keeps disappearing."

"A dog, hm?"

…Hey. Why are you looking at me?

"A dog I'm taking care of has run off several times. It happens during the night, when I'm asleep."

"An exceptionally stupid dog, then."

I told you, quit looking at me.

"That said," continued Odoro, "if it comes back every time, it may just be imposing on someone else. Although I would imagine it's a terrible nuisance for them."

…Fine, say whatever you want.

"No, she doesn't come back… Every time she disappears, I look and look for her, and eventually I find her. She's missing right now; she's been gone for half a month already."

"Half a month? That's quite a long time."

"Yes, but I've found her unexpectedly after a month before."

"Have you contacted any animal shelters?"

"Well, they never seem to take me seriously."

According to Suzu, the dog was a small breed, and her name was "Chi." Suzu fed her twice a day, morning and evening. Chi was an indoor dog, and although Suzu let her out in the garden to play once a day, Suzu's legs and back were weak, so she wasn't able to take the dog for walks. When she took her to the local vet for her checkups, Suzu sat the dog on her chair-walker and pushed it.

Hm. So did the dog run off because she was unhappy about the situation?

"You said she runs away at night, while you're asleep. Do you have any idea how it happens?"

"Absolutely none. I make sure the windows and front door are properly shut and locked every night."

"Have you ever been awakened by a noise?"

"Well, you see… I've been taking sleeping pills for about two years now."

It started when the elderly woman who lived next door, another single lady whom Suzu had been good friends with for years, moved into a nursing home.

Suzu spent her days without anyone to talk to, yet taking classes in some sort of hobby seemed like too much trouble. She'd kept more and more to herself, and at some point, she'd stopped being able to sleep at night.

Thinking *This can't go on*, she'd spoken with her doctor about it and had been given a prescription for long-acting sleeping pills. They'd made it possible for her to sleep soundly until morning, but...

"Although I'm grateful for them, I do think they work a little too well."

Apparently, it took quite a lot of noise to rouse her. Suzu was terribly afraid that if there were a fire or an earthquake, she'd be killed in her sleep.

"There was a time when I quit taking the medicine and tried to watch the dog all night. It was bad for my heart, though, so the doctor told me to stop... As a result, I still don't know how they get out."

Huh? Seiji blinked. *"They"...?*

Had she misspoken? From what Suzu had said, it sounded as if she had only one dog.

"Have you tried caging the dog before going to bed?"

"Well, I did try it, but she still ran away. No matter how often I bring her back, she's gone the next morning."

"...Do you take your medicine before locking up for the night?"

"No. I have a routine: I get into my nightclothes and brush my teeth first, then set my alarm, then go around checking all the doors and windows. After that, once I'm all ready, I take my pills."

Odoro's eyebrows twitched. For a little while, he seemed lost in thought. "Do you use an analog alarm clock? The type with a knob on the back that you turn to set the alarm hand to the time you wish to wake up?"

"Yes, yes, that's right."

"And what time do you wake up?"

"At seven in the morning."

"Every day, consistently?"

"Yes. I thought I should keep my schedule as regular as possible."

"Hm." Odoro put a hand to his chin. "Are you away from home for long periods during the day?"

"I visit a local park every day after lunch. My doctor told me to get as much sun as I can. Lately, I've been walking around looking for Chi, though."

"Even on rainy days?"

"No. I need my walker if I'm going to walk for a long time, you know? I can't use an umbrella when I'm pushing it, so I usually wear a raincoat and go to the local library."

"And when do you return home?"

"It's always a little after seven in the evening, I think. The chime in the park rings at six. I leave the park then and stop at the supermarket on my way home, so it's usually about that time."

"...I see."

The questions finally seemed to be over.

Then Seiji, who'd been listening quietly the whole time, realized that one important point had gone unaddressed. "By the way, what breed is Chi?"

"Well, let's see. The veterinarian said she was probably a Chihuahua mix. Her coat is brown, and her lower legs are pure white, as if she's wearing socks."

Hm. That sounded really cute.

"Then she has this smushed little nose. Her face is as wrinkly as a prune, and her tail curls into a little roll."

...Or maybe not so cute?

"Wh-what are her ears like?"

"I think they hung down... Wait, no they didn't. They stood up, and they were shaped like butterflies."

What kind of dog *was* this?

"Um, what sort of coat does she have?"

"It's all curly, like a stuffed bear. Erm, you know; the foreign sort they sell at department stores."

"You mean a teddy bear?"

"Yes, like that."

...It was no use. His mental image of this dog was becoming more of a monster every second.

"How long are her legs?"

"Very short. Her torso was long, though, and she had a pointed muzzle, like a fox."

Hang on a second.

"Didn't you just say her nose was smushed?"

"…Goodness." Suzu blinked. She was quiet for a while, as if she was thinking hard. "I'm sorry. There's just so much I don't know lately…," she mumbled, sounding awkward and apologetic. Then she went as silent as a closed shell.

"Why do you want to bring the dog back home so badly?" Odoro asked.

Suzu's cheek twitched. Unease crept into her large, dark eyes. "…Why was it again?" she murmured into her coffee cup. Her gaze grew strangely distant. "Oh, that's right." She nodded, rather flatly. "There's a boy who's lonely." Her expression was vague, as if she was half-asleep. "It hurts to be all alone, you know."

The things she was saying weren't really meshing. Her eyes had grown unfocused, and she didn't even seem to see Seiji. She was looking in an entirely different direction.

"He left her with me, you see. I felt as if I had to take care of her properly. He was counting on me. I felt like I mustn't die yet, for their sakes. And yet, and yet, she disappeared. So I thought, 'I have to hurry and find her.'"

Her wrinkled hands were so tense, it hurt to look at them. Her knuckles had gone white. Seiji realized that the coffee in her half-full cup was sloshing so dramatically that it threatened to spill over.

She's shaking.

"Um, Suzu…"

Unable to just sit by and watch, Seiji had started to call to her, when—

Odoro snapped his fingers sharply.

Blinking as if he'd startled her, Suzu glanced around. "Goodness. Where am I?" She looked like a lost child. Her face showed confusion and unease, and she appeared disgusted with and disappointed in herself. She seemed to have completely forgotten why she was here. "Oh dear, how awful. I wonder why I imposed on you… Goodness gracious, you've even treated me to coffee. I'm so sorry. I hope I haven't made a nuisance of myself."

"It's all right. You came to speak with me about your dog, and I've accepted your request." Odoro's voice was perfectly calm. He seemed to have said the words specifically to reassure her.

Suzu looked back at him steadily. Then, without warning, her face crumpled. "Oh, I'm so glad. I've wanted to talk to someone about it so very badly. I just don't know what to do with them anymore. Thank you so much for your help." She bowed deeply.

However, when she raised her head, her expression had changed yet again. Her eyes had gone vague. She smiled brightly at Odoro, as if they'd been making small talk. "I should be going. I'm not sure who you are, but you've been very kind to this old woman, and I appreciate it very much."

The word that skimmed across Seiji's mind sent a chill down his spine. *Dementia.*

"Will you go straight home?" Odoro asked.

Suzu cocked her head like a finch. "Let's see… I think I'll stop by the library, then pick up something to eat from the supermarket deli. According to the weather forecast, the rain's supposed to get stronger."

"…I'd recommend delaying your return home for as long as possible today."

"Oh? Why is that?"

"Because it will make it easier to find the dog."

Now *there* was a significant-sounding statement.

Like Seiji, Suzu looked dubious. Rising from the sofa with some effort, she bowed deeply to Odoro. "Please do take care." As she tried to board the elevator, her chair-walker's wheels caught in the gap, stalling her.

Odoro promptly got up. "Let me help you."

"Gracious, that's sweet of you."

In an unexpected display of kindness, Odoro caught the end of the chair-walker and lifted it one-handed, shifting it into the elevator with ease. Then he helped the appreciative, embarrassed Suzu in, and the elevator started to descend.

...I didn't see that coming. Seiji had just assumed this guy was violence and sadism incarnate, someone with a completely busted personality. But it seemed he had an unexpectedly chivalrous side.

Impressed, Seiji quickly tried to sit down on the empty sofa, but...

"Dwah!"

He pitched forward and fell. Odoro had stuck out a leg and tripped him.

"Beg pardon," Odoro said, without even looking at him. For just a moment, he frowned slightly, as if he was concerned about having soiled the toe of his shoe. Then he promptly reclaimed his seat on the sofa. "...This is very strange."

"*Go bald right this second,*" Seiji cursed him under his breath. Giving up on the sofa, he sat on the floor, hugging his knees. Then he thought about the exchange he'd just heard. "Was that what they call 'sundowning'? We should contact somebody who's close to her, instead of looking for her dog. Maybe the local welfare commissioner, or at least someone who'll be her friend..."

If her dog kept running away, it was probably just because she was forgetting to lock up. This sounded like a job for a clinic or the neighborhood association, not a detective.

However, Odoro gave him a look that seemed to say, *Who would have believed this dog could talk?* "I see. So this is what happens when fools speak."

...Who does he think he is anyway? Some kind of prince? I suppose he is, come to think of it...

"Hm," Odoro muttered. "That was five breeds." He tapped his index finger on the arm of the sofa. "The dog characteristics that Suzu gave correspond to a Chihuahua, a pug, a papillon, a toy poodle, and a dachshund—the only common trait is that they are all small breeds."

Huh? What exactly was he talking about? Seiji had no idea.

Um, so basically, he picked up on something from what Suzu said?

When Seiji was with Shiroshi, he tended to forget, but Odoro was the one who was publicly treated as a great detective. Seiji always got the urge to label him second-class, but perhaps the man was actually competent.

Getting up, Odoro went over to the study space at the back of the loft.

Opening one of the desk's locked drawers, he took something out and slipped it into his jacket. It looked like a revolver to Seiji—but surely he must have been seeing things.

Then Odoro took a fedora off the desktop, placed it on his head, and picked up the walking stick that had been leaning against the desk. "We're going out."

"Huh?"

"Since the Enma Ministry sent that notice, I suppose I'll need to take you with me."

With a sigh, he set off, shoes clicking on the floor. He was fast.

What is this, competitive walking?! Seiji didn't have time to even grouse about it; hastily running after Odoro, he slid into the elevator at the very last second. There was a *ding*, and it promptly deposited them on the first floor.

It was about half past four. They were pretty close to the hour of demons, but the sky was still gray and drizzling, and it made the boundary between daytime and sunset hard to pin down.

"Now then. We're going to pay a visit to the client's residence."

"Huh? But we don't know her address or anything."

Odoro's hand came up smoothly. It was holding a postcard; a direct mail ad from a dry cleaning place. The name of the addressee was—Suzu Torikai.

Did he steal that?!

It must have happened when Suzu was trying to board the elevator. When he'd moved her chair-walker, he'd probably snitched this from the side pocket.

Before Seiji could press the issue, Odoro hailed a taxi and they headed for the address on the postcard. It turned out to belong to a house in a blue-collar residential district crowded with similar houses.

It was a small place: a run-down, single-story wooden house. The garden was bordered by an old-fashioned cinder block wall and planted modestly with trees that were already winter bare.

The sign on the gatepost read TORIKAI. This was Suzu's house.

Without hesitation, Odoro rang the doorbell. There was no response: She was still out. *What now?* Seiji thought, watching the situation develop as though it had nothing to do with him.

"...We'll try the back entrance." Odoro strode through the gate; Seiji followed him timidly. They went around the house, passing a rack with laundry poles, and discovered the back door next to the external air-conditioning unit.

Odoro tried the knob. Naturally, it was locked. *What now?* Seiji was wondering again, when—

Bam!

—Odoro kicked the door down. It might have been badly hung to begin with; the hinges flew right off.

"Wh-what are you doing?!" Seiji was starting to protest when a stink rolled out from inside that made him shut his mouth and cover his nose.

Yikes, what's that stench?!

It smelled like something was rotting.

Odoro sniffed audibly. Then with a still, perfectly blank face, he said: "The other side of the house...most likely in the kitchen."

What are you, a dog? Seiji retorted mentally. Ignoring him, Odoro walked in without taking his shoes off, as if that were the natural thing to do. This was flagrant breaking and entering. If someone called it in, the two of them would be arrested on the spot, no questions asked.

Dammit! If it happens, it happens. Kicking off his shoes rather desperately, Seiji sneaked in after Odoro. The door opened onto a narrow hallway. There was a tiny bathroom on the left, and what seemed to be a kitchen at the end.

Seiji groped his way carefully along the wall, feeling for a light switch. "Oh, found it."

When he flipped the switch, the lights came on, revealing a simple kitchen.

Pots and frying pans hung on the tiled walls. At first glance, everything seemed to be well used, carefully maintained, and pleasantly neat, except...

"...Something really does seem a little off here, doesn't it?"

The window glass was all dusty, and a dead potted pothos sat in front of it. When Seiji looked closer, the sink was cloudy with limescale, and there were empty deli packs stacked in it. A small mountain of plastic garbage bags were piled against one wall; Suzu had probably forgotten to put them out on garbage day.

More than anything, there was that smell.

Maybe she's let the contents of the fridge go rotten because of her dementia?

Just as that thought occurred to Seiji, his eyes found the refrigerator. *No, I seriously can't open that*, he thought, deciding to pretend he hadn't seen it. But as he was sidling away from it...

"Don't run." Odoro glared at him menacingly, his nose wrinkling like a mad dog's.

Jesus.

However...

"Huh?"

He'd just assumed the fridge would be packed with rotten, oozing meat and fish, but it was empty. She must get most of her meals from the deli.

"What? But then where's the smell coming from?"

Just then, a small black shape skittered past his feet, and Seiji jumped. *Cockroach?!* he thought, but it wasn't. It was a rather flat beetle; that part was the same, but this one had shorter feelers, and its body was boxy.

"It appears to be a carrion beetle," Odoro murmured. "Also known as a burying beetle. They're notorious scavengers that feed on animal corpses."

Wh-what's with that extremely ominous description? Seiji shuddered.

The carrion beetle scuttled across the wooden floor until it reached the sink, and then...

"Oh? What's this?"

There was a small square set of double doors in the floor. Apparently, the kitchen had an under-floor storage space.

The carrion beetle promptly squeezed through the crack between the doors. It was acting as if it had found its meal. That's right, carrion beetles could trace the smell of death to its source.

"...I see," said Odoro. "Here, hm?"

"No, um, just a second, I'm not ready for— Yaaaaaaugh!"

No sooner had Odoro pulled the doors open than a cloud of black specks exploded into the room.

Flies.

Instantly, the stench punched Seiji in the nose.

He'd opened his mouth to scream, and flies seemed to scramble over themselves to get into it. He flailed his arms frantically.

What surfaced from the fetid darkness were the rotting corpses of dogs.

The eyes seemed to have dissolved already; white maggots crawled in and out of the gaping sockets. Then there were the black swarming carrion beetles... The space had become a den of insects.

The stink seemed liable to twist Seiji's nose off, and he groaned. He clapped a hand over his mouth, just barely managing to swallow what was threatening to come up. *What the heck is going on here?* Shaking his thoroughly confused head, he involuntarily backed away.

"Pug, papillon, toy poodle, dachshund... Hm. There's one missing," Odoro said. He was looking down into the hole in the floor, his profile unreadable. "In short, there were five dogs that Suzu called 'Chi.'"

Seiji didn't understand what he was hearing. Guessing as much from his expression, Odoro snorted, as if he found this tiresome. "The one with the wrinkled face was a pug. The butterfly ears belonged to the papillon, the one with the curly coat was a toy poodle, and the one with short legs was a dachshund. When Suzu described 'Chi' to us, she mixed traits from all of those breeds together."

"Huh? But why would she...?"

"The first 'Chi' was probably the Chihuahua mix. When her pet disappeared, Suzu was upset and searched all over for her. Then she got it into her head that another small dog who looked nothing like her was 'Chi' and brought it home."

"Then these dogs were...?"

"Either abandoned or lost," Odoro said. His voice was casual, but his uncharacteristically melancholy profile seemed to be quietly mourning the dogs' deaths.

"Who would do a thing like…?" Seiji started to say, and then an awful possibility occurred to him. "It can't have been Suzu, can it?" A pleading note crept into his voice.

If Suzu had killed the dogs she brought home one after another, hidden their bodies under the floor, then forgotten about them, the situation would be far too bleak.

"There's very little possibility of that. According to Suzu, the dogs always disappear during the night, after she's taken her medication and is fast asleep."

"B-but how could she miss this stench?"

"A dulled sense of smell is an early symptom of Alzheimer's. In addition, the human nose grows accustomed to bad smells easily. It wouldn't have been odd for her to go about her days without noticing it."

But what if Suzu's dementia had caused her to sleepwalk, and she was killing the dogs while she slept…?

"You've seen too many horror movies."

"But I mean, she lives by herself, doesn't she? Then who did this?"

"I believe that is what we are here to find out." Shrugging, Odoro strode into the next room. Hastily shutting the storage compartment's doors, Seiji followed him.

Beyond a retro bead curtain, there was a tatami-floored room about ten meters square. It was a good old-fashioned living room, complete with a TV and a low tea table. There was a set of glass patio doors in the far wall; a slice of oddly vivid darkness showed through the crack between their closed curtains. The sound of the rain had grown louder. Apparently, it had started coming down in earnest.

"Um… Oh, there we go."

Seiji tugged the string of the overhead fluorescent light, and the room brightened.

There was a sliding door in the wall to the left coming from the kitchen, with a small traditional chest of drawers at its edge. Odoro stood in front of it, gazing down at its top. When Seiji looked, it was thinly coated with dust.

…Huh?

There was a small clear rectangle in that dust. It was as if an object had been sitting there until just recently.

"Um, what's…?" he was about to ask, when something abruptly started making noise.

Bzz-bzz-bzz-bzz-bzz.

Seiji jumped. Looking around, he spotted a floor cushion in the shadow of the low table, folded in two. The muffled alarm was coming from inside it.

"Huh? Don't tell me…"

But when he pulled the object out, sure enough, it was an analog alarm clock. The alarm hand was pointing to a few minutes before six.

Five fifty—that was right now.

What was this about?

Seiji was pretty sure Suzu had said she set her alarm for seven AM every night. That would mean she'd intentionally reset it to this time. That was weird, though. It wasn't as if anyone was supposed to be here right now.

Hm?

For just a moment, he thought he saw Odoro smirk faintly, but the expression was gone before he could even blink.

"Hey. Underdog."

Dammit. Does he think I'll respond to that or something?

"…What?"

"If you're bored, go investigate the back, please. I'm going to step outside to place a phone call." Taking his flip phone from inside his jacket, Odoro jerked his chin toward a second bead curtain. A gloomy hallway lay behind it.

Heck no. Screw that.

Seiji would have loved to respectfully decline, using those exact words, but he was too scared of what would happen if he did. With an earnest prayer in his heart—*please let this jerk get chewed on by a* nue *again someday*—he trudged out of the living room. The bead curtain rattled as he passed through it. There was a door set with a pane of frosted glass on the left side of the hall.

Um, that's probably either the washroom or the bath.

Nervously grasping the knob, he opened the door slowly, peeking in through the crack.

A nasty feeling came over him.

Was it…eyes? He felt as if he were being watched. It was the same gaze he felt on his back from out of nowhere when he was washing himself before getting into the bath, late at night. In the end, it was always just his imagination, but…

For now, let's get the lights on.

Desperately feeling along the wall, he flipped the switch. A fluorescent light flashed on overhead.

"Eep!"

There was a stainless steel sliding door in front of him, probably the door to the bath. In the frosted glass of the top half, he'd seen the vague silhouette of a figure.

But…

"…Oh. It's me, huh?"

Realizing that the figure looked just like his own, he sighed in relief. The room on the other side was dark, and apparently, the fluorescent light had reflected off the frosted glass, turning it into an impromptu mirror.

Still, that really is creepy.

Only after he'd awkwardly turned his back on it was he able to focus on observing the room around him.

It was probably a combination dressing room and washroom. The wood-floored space was cramped to begin with, and it seemed just as cluttered as the kitchen. A big bottle of laundry detergent that looked as if it was probably for commercial use sat right in the middle of the floor.

On the mirrored washstand, there was a single toothbrush in a cup on the rim of the sink. He saw a tube of toothpaste that had been accidentally left uncapped and a hairbrush with some stray white hairs tangled in it.

There was a twin tub washing machine that looked like a relic from several decades back. A melancholy, forgotten load of laundry lay all dried up in the bottom.

He didn't see anything particularly abnormal, though. Not that he had any idea what he was supposed to investigate or how...

I guess the bath is next?

He turned to face the sliding door at the back of the room again, and then...

"Huh?"

Somewhere in his head, an alarm bell began to ring.

Something was wrong.

He didn't know what, though. These premonitions were more like wild instinct anyway, something far removed from intelligence or thought. However, unless you figured out what was causing them fast, they always ended in disaster.

"Oh."

The moment he noticed it, he felt his temperature plummet.

There was no shadow.

The human silhouette that he'd seen in the glass wasn't there now. It had definitely been there a minute ago, and Seiji had just assumed it was his own reflection, but...

...come to think of it...

...he'd heard that glass showed reflections because its smooth surface reflected the light, but the surface of frosted glass was covered in tiny bumps and dips. Could it even reflect anything?

Then was that...?

Had someone been standing in the bathroom, on the other side of that glass? Had they been looking through the upper half of the door, just as he'd done from this side?

Seiji swallowed hard.

Timidly setting a hand on the sliding door, he started to open it and peek in through the gap, when...

In the distance, a chime began to play. It was probably coming from the disaster prevention speakers in the park—a warped, cracked version of "Yuuyake Koyake."

And then…

…the door rattled open, and an arm shot out and grabbed Seiji's shirtfront.

It happened all at once, in the space of a moment so brief that he didn't even have time to blink. What he saw seemed to move in slow motion.

The owner of the arm was a young guy about Seiji's age. Bloodshot eyes glared at him through shaggy, overgrown bangs.

Suddenly, his assailant turned into a hideous man with a shaved head. Three hairy fingers raked the air hungrily, and a long tongue snaked out of his mouth.

Promptly reverting to normal, the arm yanked Seiji's shirt, hauling him into the bathroom. Seiji pitched forward, reflexively planting his hands on the tiled floor.

Something whistled through the air.

Uh-oh. He twisted around to look up. The young guy was standing right above him, and he'd just raised something high over his head.

It looked like—a clock. A clearly retro, weighty, solid-looking clock made of marble. Right, *the sort that could probably kill you with one blow to the skull.*

"Don't—!" Seiji rolled, evading at the last second, but the clock struck his shoulder instead. A pain like pins and needles lanced through his whole arm, and he groaned, clamping a hand over his shoulder. He didn't even have time to thrash around on the floor, though. His attacker promptly grabbed his collar, hauled him up, and slammed his head into the edge of the bathtub.

A scorched smell flooded his nose, and his vision went black. He nearly passed out but managed to stay conscious.

He'd come down on his back, and the other guy straddled him and began throttling him for all he was worth.

The man's thumbs sank into his throat, squeezing a croaking groan out of it. Blood churned in the depths of Seiji's ears, roaring, and his whole face flushed hot.

Dammit, I have to get Odoro's attention, and he's outside!

He needed to scream or bang on something and call for help.

Except...

...Hang on.

Why had Odoro gone outside in the first place? To make a phone call. That sounded like a perfectly decent excuse, but would a guy like him care about fine etiquette like avoiding phone calls in public? Especially on a night so rainy that umbrellas were basically mandatory.

Don't tell me..., he thought, as memory fragments began to surface, one after another.

That smirk on Odoro's face, just before he'd told Seiji to search the back of the house. Had he been gazing steadily at that chest of drawers because he'd noticed the mark where the clock had been?

Did he know this was going to happen?

Seiji didn't understand the detailed reasoning behind it. However, if Odoro had somehow realized that someone was lurking in the house, guessed their hiding place, then sent Seiji to them...

Then he'd gone outside *in order to let Seiji get killed*. To make sure he died where he couldn't see him, so that it wouldn't violate his agreement with Takamura.

Damn that bastard!

For a moment, anger nearly dyed Seiji's vision red, but now wasn't the time. Unless he did something, he was going to die. That was a fact. He absolutely couldn't let that happen.

This is the second time somebody's almost killed me.

The first was when Serina chased him around with a carving knife.

But back then, frankly, somewhere in his mind, he'd been resigned to it. He hadn't wanted to feel pain or suffer or go through something awful, so he hadn't wanted to die. That said, he'd figured that if this was the end, then it was the end, and there wasn't much he could do about it.

He hadn't lived seriously enough that he'd be left with regrets if his life was abruptly cut short.

In fact, that hadn't even been the half of it.

I had nothing.

No house, no money, no job, no friends, not even a place to belong or anywhere to go.

Nothing.

He'd really had nothing at all.

Well, he still had practically nothing. That part was the same.

But now...

...he had Shiroshi. At the very least, he had someone who said he needed him.

And right now, he didn't know whether Shiroshi was dead or alive.

No regret could possibly be bigger than that.

Groping around, Seiji found his phone in his back pocket and slammed it into the other guy's face as hard as he could. He'd managed to score a direct hit on his nose, and for a second, the fingers around his throat went limp.

Seiji grabbed the chance to crawl out from under his attacker. As the guy got to his feet, holding his nose, Seiji body-slammed him, and they tumbled into the tub, tangling together.

The other guy had ended up on the bottom, and he started kicking like mad. As Seiji desperately reached for the rim of the bathtub, his hand happened to connect with the faucet. Taking a gamble, he turned it. It had been switched to the shower, and a jet of water erupted from the showerhead, hitting his attacker in the face.

The guy had almost managed to stand, but the force of the water made his feet slip and sent him back to the bottom of the tub. He hastily tried to get up, but the running water made it hard for him to get any traction.

Grabbing his chance, Seiji bolted out of the tub.

He tumbled through the open sliding door into the washroom, then tripped over something and crashed to the floor.

Meanwhile, in the bathroom...

Finally managing to find the tap, the guy shut off the shower. He heard a thud from the washroom, then a rattle as someone ran through the bead curtain. His opponent had fled into the living room.

Swearing, the guy hit the faucet in a fit of anger. A trickle of blood dribbled from his nose. He wiped it off with the back of his hand, as if it irritated him, then climbed out of the tub, staggering a little.

He stood in the washroom, peeking out into the hall.

There were no sounds, no sign that anyone was there. His opponent seemed to have escaped outside.

When he looked through the open door toward the living room, the bead curtain that separated it from the hall was still swaying slightly.

There was no other movement. *So he really did run for it?*

Exhaling in relief, he stepped out into the hall, starting toward the living room, and then…

…he heard something whistle through the air.

Before the guy could turn around, Seiji brought a big four-kilogram bottle of laundry detergent down on the back of his head.

There was a *whunk*, and the guy crumpled to the floor at Seiji's feet. His eyes rolled back so far that their whites showed. He was out cold.

The trick had been a very simple one.

When Seiji fled into the washroom, he'd tripped over that big bottle of detergent. He'd grabbed it and bolted out into the hall, smacked the bead curtain to make it rattle as loudly as possible, then flattened himself against the wall by the door and waited for the other guy to come out.

Seiji might not look it, but he'd learned a thing or two after coming through so many ugly situations.

After all, when he took a part-time job, four times out of ten, it ended with him getting run off and told not to come back. Some of those times had ended in violence, and once—when he'd worked at a sketchy bar—he'd ended up in a hellish game of chase with its golf club–brandishing proprietor. He was going to have to take the reason for that one to his grave, however.

Still, this is the first time I've ever hit back.

Gritting his teeth against the pain in his joints, he looked down at the other guy. The man looked like a beached dolphin or whale; he wasn't even twitching.

Don't tell me he's dead...

Seiji carefully put his ear next to the guy's mouth and was relieved to hear surprisingly steady breathing.

But who the heck was this?

Considering the circumstances, he'd definitely been lurking in the house before Seiji and Odoro got there. Suzu had said she lived alone, though. There was only one toothbrush by the sink, and he didn't see a razor anywhere. The guy probably wasn't a family member who lived with her.

He might have something to do with the dog corpses under the floor, though.

Still...for some reason, he reminds me of somebody.

The collar of his jacket was black with grime, and the heels of his sneakers were worn down so far that they'd developed holes. His hollow cheeks were pale, and the circles under his eyes were as dark as soot. His face looked as if he was tired of living altogether.

Oh, I see... He looked exactly like Seiji had ten months ago, when he'd been wandering between net cafés, pursued by loan sharks.

Um... For now, I guess I'll tie him up.

It was just a chance resemblance, after all. There was no guarantee the other guy wouldn't try to strangle him again. Restraining him now was probably the best move.

On that thought, Seiji hooked his hands under the guy's armpits and dragged him into the living room. As he was wondering, *Should I look for some packing twine or use an extension cord as a rope?...*

"Oh."

...he made eye contact with Odoro. At some point, the man had come back, and he was standing glumly in the living room. He crossed his arms with a loud, irritated *tch*. "You're unexpectedly stubborn."

Seiji's resentment peaked. *Okay, that does it. I'm done willing him to go bald. Someday, I swear I'll rip his hair out myself.* As he was making that private resolution…

"And?"

"Excuse me?"

"What sort of yokai did he resemble?"

Like I'd tell you, dumbass. The words were on the tip of his tongue, but then he thought of Suzu and the dogs and choked them back down. After he'd grudgingly explained…

"I see. *Himamushi nyuudou*, hm?" Odoro said, surprisingly quickly. "'When one squanders his time and spends his life in idleness, upon his death, his spirit becomes a *himamushi nyuudou*.' It's a yokai depicted in Toriyama Sekien's *More of the Demon Horde from Past and Present.* As the word '*nyuudou*' indicates, it takes the shape of a man with a shaved head. However, it's actually a cockroach in human form."

In the Chinese *Compendium of Materia Medica*, male cockroaches were called "*himushi*" or "*hitorimushi*," "fire" or "lantern" bugs.

"In addition, the name is considered to be a pun: Although the characters used to write the word are different, the '*hima*' in '*himamushi*' can be interpreted as the word for 'idleness,' while '*mushi*' is a homonym for a word that means to spend one's life in vain, doing nothing. To that end, Sekien interprets it as 'what one who spends their life being terribly lazy and useless becomes after death.'

"Cockroaches lurk in the darkness, avoiding the light, and infest others' homes. They creep through the house behind its residents' backs, scavenging their leftovers and finally consuming the house itself. And…" Odoro glanced down at the young man at his feet. From the expression in his eyes, he could have been looking at an actual insect. "Like a cockroach, this man crept into Suzu's house. During the day, while she was at the park or the supermarket, and at night, when she'd taken her medication and was sound asleep, he'd nap in the living room, use the bath and the toilet, and graze on the deli leftovers in the kitchen. He was a parasite in her home."

From the look of the guy, he was probably homeless.

He'd somehow gotten his hands on the key to Suzu's house. Adjusting his habits to match its resident's daily rhythms, he'd infiltrated her house and used it to partially cover his needs for food, clothing, and shelter.

"It was the alarm clock that gave him away. If Suzu was telling the truth, she was in the habit of turning the knob on the back and setting the alarm before going to bed every night. However, that doesn't make any sense."

"Huh? Why?"

"If she woke at seven every morning, there should have been no need to reset the alarm."

An involuntary "Oh" escaped Seiji. That was true: If she always got up at the same time, she shouldn't have had to do anything except switch the alarm on.

"I presume that when he crept in during the day, he folded a floor cushion in half, put the clock inside it, and napped. He set the alarm to wake him just before Suzu left the park, at five fifty PM. That is why Suzu was compelled to reset her alarm every night."

I see.

"It's likely that the dogs were killed because they threatened his parasitic lifestyle. Every time Suzu mistook a dog for 'Chi' and brought it home, he killed it during the night and hid it beneath the floor."

Suzu had assumed the missing dog had run away, and she'd walked all around the neighborhood, searching for it for days and days, months on end. Until at last she grew so worried that she went to a detective agency for advice.

"…How cruel," Seiji murmured.

Behind him, there was a shriek. The young guy had bolted up and was sitting weakly on the tatami, clearly confused. His lips were trembling.

Slowly, Odoro turned his head. On seeing the man, he gave a mocking smile. There was naked, brutish sadism in his expression.

Then he thumped the end of his walking stick on the floor.

"Come."

With a bang, the doors of the under-floor storage space flew open.

The shadows of four-legged animals leaped out. There were four of them.

Each one was small—so short, it didn't even come up to Seiji's knee. Their ferocious, gaping mouths were filled with long black fangs.

Howls went up. The creatures sounded like hounds, bellowing to announce the start of the hunt.

It was a terribly surreal sight, and the young intruder stared in shock.

"Wh-what are those? What the hell are those?!"

"*Sunekosuri.* Originally, each was a dog you killed. Even if you die, I won't let you claim you've forgotten."

Odoro snapped his fingers.

"Hunt."

He had just passed judgment. A fall into Hell, to punish the guilty.

"Eep— EeeeEEEEE!"

With a confused, terrified scream, the guy sprinted out of the living room. Passing right by the shoe cupboard in the entryway, he lunged for the doorknob, then dashed into the street.

The pack of dogs took off after him.

They disappeared the moment they raced through the front door, but their footsteps were still audible. So was their rough panting as they ran with all their might.

Invisible dogs, dashing down a street half hidden by a downpour: That was probably what *sunekosuri* were really like.

And then...

"...Huh?"

Sensing a presence, Seiji turned. A small shadow had emerged from the living room and was making for the front door on unsteady feet.

There's the fifth one.

"Hm. That was probably the first. The Chihuahua mix whose corpse was not under the floor. Even if its body isn't there, something like the emotions it felt when it died seem to have remained. It's what one would call a ghost."

"Then that's..."

Was this "Chi," Suzu's original dog?

Resentment or anger—a thirst for revenge on the one who'd killed them—was probably what was driving the five dogs. Something so intense that even killing the guy wouldn't be enough.

It serves him right...probably.

Seiji shook his head, feeling dismal, and then...

"Oh!" he yelped. In what felt like a flash of intuition, a possibility had struck him. "W-wait... Wait just a minute!" Forcing the wheels in his head to turn, Seiji desperately groped for words. "That guy—he might not have been all bad."

Come to think of it, considering the circumstances, that man had probably been napping when Odoro demolished the back door. A suspicious pair had tromped into the home of an old woman who lived by herself while she was out, without even bothering to take off their shoes. They were clearly thieves or robbers. If he was thinking of his own safety, running would have been his first choice. In fact, since he'd had his shoes on, he might have originally planned to flee through the front door.

And yet...

Ultimately, he'd chosen to grab the clock from the dresser and hide in the washroom. He'd actually turned and gone back into the house.

If he did it for Suzu...

The man had known Suzu left the park when the "Yuuyake Koyake" chime played. He must have realized that if she came home unawares, she'd run right into the intruders.

Was he...worried about her?

If that was why he'd stayed in the house—to see how the situation played out, just in case—it would mean he'd been trying to save her.

When he heard Seiji's argument, Odoro raised an eyebrow. "I see." And then he spat, "*What of it?*"

Hauling Seiji up by his shirtfront, he pushed his face in close, like a beast about to snap at Seiji's nose.

"Yes, you're right. That man may have meant to save the old woman he was sponging off of. So are you implying that I should forgive his crime and grant him an opportunity to atone because of it? Like that half-breed would? Ha! You two are most definitely the heretics here." His voice was threatening. "As a rule, Hell's punishment doesn't require the possibility of mercy. In the face of the sin that has been committed, there is no room to make allowances."

In contrast, his eyes were endlessly sober, so devoid of emotion that they seemed hollow.

"After all, to its victims, a crime is always just a crime. No matter how the sinner atones, it's essentially impossible for the sin and its penance to balance each other out. For that reason, all sinners have a duty to be punished."

After all, the one thing no one could ever do was resurrect the dead. That was why those who had been victimized prayed, *At least punish the one who did this.*

"If an apology were enough, there would quite literally be no need for Hell."

Seiji had no response to give him. Odoro was right: There were sins that could never be mended, no matter what. No matter how much room for sympathy there might be in that man's case, the dogs he'd killed wouldn't come back to life.

Even so…

Knocking Odoro's hand away, Seiji retrieved the shoes he'd kicked off at the back door and ran out into the rainy street. He had no idea which way the man had gone, though.

I really do get it, Seiji murmured to himself. He slapped his cheeks, shaking off his hesitation.

Odoro was undeniably in the right here.

However, even if everyone else cursed the guy as a dog killer and threw rocks at his back, Seiji couldn't just look the other way. He'd been that guy once.

If he hadn't met Shiroshi, he was sure he would have ended up as something similar. He couldn't rationalize this away as someone else's problem.

After all, somebody saved me.

Desperately hoping for some kind of hint, he got out his phone and opened its browser, but a search for "*sunekosuri*" turned up very little.

Something like a dog that slips through the legs of passersby on rainy evenings. That was it.

"Gaaaah, dammit!"

With a yell that was very like a howl, Seiji dashed off into the rain.

…Alone.

*

His mother's mood set the tone of every single day.

For as far back as Kazushi Migiwa could remember, that had been his life.

To a casual observer, they'd probably seemed like the sort of family one could find anywhere: a mother devoted to education and to her timid, serious only son.

To Kazushi, the pair were more like a warden and her prisoner.

When he got home from elementary school, his mother would tutor him one-on-one.

No, *tutor* wasn't the word. It had been nothing that gentle. As his monitor, she'd sat with him until so late at night, it was technically morning. If he dozed off even briefly, she'd hit his head with the textbook and dash tea into his face.

"Why must you make me angry?!" she always said.

When Kazushi silently submitted to her scolding, she'd rebuke him with "Why don't you say something?! Answer me!"

Then he'd be locked in the bathroom all night. The eyes of the neighbors were probably the only reason she didn't shut him out of the house. He had water to drink, at least, but it was freezing cold in winter, and at night, the room was pitch-black.

In an attempt to warm up a little, he'd sit on the heated toilet seat, hugging his knees. At times like that, he felt as if his body would either dissolve into the darkness or become a corpse.

If only that would happen, Kazushi thought, *it would make everything easier.*

Even so, he kept earning the highest grades in his classes, right up until the end of his last year of middle school. He made it into the best escalator school in the prefecture, but it wasn't long before he stopped being able to attend.

Every time he got into his uniform and stood in the entryway, his body grew terribly heavy. No matter how his mother cursed at him or hit him, he couldn't make his feet take a single step.

He became a shut-in and stopped attending school. And now that it had happened, he felt as if he'd always known he'd end up like this. He'd never meshed with the rest of the world. He felt like he'd been born not as a human but as some other, worthless creature.

At first, his mother made frequent trips to the school to talk with the counselor and Kazushi's homeroom teacher. When they decided to expel him, she tried desperately to make him attend cram school for the high school equivalency exam. And finally, Kazushi became something that simply didn't exist.

Just like his father.

His father worked at a government office. He'd come home at ten on the dot every night, have an evening drink with whatever leftovers happened to be in the fridge, and stare vacantly at the television.

Hearing a child crying in the bathroom all night long didn't seem to bother him. He'd just do his business in a plastic bottle instead. At this point, when Kazushi tried to picture his face, all he could remember was the fact that his tortoiseshell glasses had always been cloudy with fingerprints.

If you switched the TV for a computer, Kazushi was about the same.

The only difference was that his mother wouldn't even tolerate the sight of Kazushi. Just being there was enough to get him railed at, hit, taunted, and crushed.

It was as if he were a cockroach in human form.

At some point, Kazushi took to waiting until his mother went to bed, before crawling out of his room and raiding the fridge to fill his belly and keep himself alive. He was a pest who lived in the shadows of the house.

After five years had passed, he ran into his mother in the kitchen late one night.

A bag of prescription medicine had been tossed carelessly onto the table. The name of the hospital printed on the side told him she was a patient of the behavioral health department. There was nothing Kazushi could say to her, though.

He'd turned his back on the fluorescent light and was trying to blend into the gloom of the hallway when he heard a tuneless, singsong voice.

"Good boy, good boy, good-for-nothing boy."

It was his mother. She was sitting at the table, head drooping, gazing steadily at the prescription bag.

"You steal into the kitchen late at night to scavenge food, and when the light comes on, you run. You're just like a cockroach."

Then she looked at him. Hatred, resentment, contempt—she'd taken all the emotions ready to explode out of her and converted them into tears that ran down her cheeks.

"To think this thing is my child."

And then…

"Why are you alive?"

Don't look at me.

The next thing Kazushi knew, he'd hauled off and punched her cheek with everything he had.

His mother went over sideways, falling out of her chair and hitting the floor hard.

She fixed him with a frightened glare; her face had gone past pale white to blackish. Was it anger, shock, or fear? He couldn't tell from her eyes.

Once he'd hit her, though, he couldn't stop.

He choked her, punched her, kicked her.

His father had apparently come home right at ten as usual, but although he saw his son straddling his mother and beating her and heard his wife scream, "Help me! He's going to kill me!" he just spent all night staring vaguely at the TV.

The next morning, his mother crawled out the front door, and she never came back. Kazushi left the house two weeks later.

He'd come home just once after that.

Maybe his parents had ended up divorcing. The house was just an empty shell with a FOR SALE sign on it.

After that, he went into free-fall.

It was as if he'd stumbled through a trapdoor: He fell headlong, with no way to stop.

At first, he lived out of net cafés and tried to find a job through Hello Work and help-wanted magazines. He was a high school dropout who'd only completed middle school, though. He had no fixed address, no ID, and no one to act as his guarantor. With such a wealth of "nothing," he had no chance of finding decent work.

He managed to register on a smartphone help-wanted site and find day labor gigs at warehouses and factories, but every job was inundated with applicants. He was lucky if he got two days of work a week.

As his money dwindled, his clothes developed sweat stains, and his greasy hair started to smell pretty rank. Since he didn't have a decent place to sleep, there were always dark circles under his eyes, and his mind was hazy around the clock.

He had no house, no money, and no job.

His life was worthless.

He had nothing.

In search of a place to sleep, he eventually wound up at a small park.

The park was like a hole in the middle of the city: It had a slide, a bench that seated two, and a drinking fountain, but that was all.

In the evening, "Yuuyake Koyake" chimed from the disaster prevention speaker, but there were no children around to hear it. No one even walked by.

All of this was convenient for Kazushi.

One day in April, he'd washed his face and head in the drinking fountain and was lying on the bench when a dog appeared out of nowhere. It was a Chihuahua mix. Since it didn't have a collar, it was probably a stray or a dog somebody had abandoned.

It put its front paws up on the bench, sniffing at Kazushi with its moist nose.

When Kazushi sat up, it backed away but looked up at him with steady, searching eyes. It didn't seem suspicious but rather like it wasn't sure whether it should wag its tail. Almost involuntarily, Kazushi put out his hand; the dog sniffed it, then nuzzled it.

"...Are you hungry?"

When he tore off some of his stuffed roll and held it out, the dog ate it, smacking its tongue noisily. It must have been famished. When it was done eating, it put its front paws on Kazushi's knees and licked his face all around his nose, wagging its tail so hard that it seemed like it might come right off.

From that point on, the park had two residents: one human, one canine.

Kazushi fed the dog because he felt like it; it could take its leave and go elsewhere anytime it wanted to. His attitude toward it was careless, but the dog didn't leave his side.

It was always beetling around, digging holes in the sandbox or sticking its head into the weeds and smelling all the scents. Its gait was oddly unsteady, though, and it had a habit of pestering Kazushi to pick it up when there was even a small step to climb.

When Kazushi called, "Hey," it whipped around to look at him and wag its tail. Then it would run up to him as fast as it could, sniff his outstretched hand, then jump into his arms and lick his nose and lips.

Kazushi took to calling it Chako, or "brown girl."

The reason was simple: The dog was brown and a female.

Once he'd named her, though, that dog was Kazushi's. Even though he knew he didn't really have the right to own a dog.

Still, whenever he called "Chako," the dog wagged her tail. When he tapped her lightly on the head or petted her back, she snuffled happily.

In June, with summer just around the corner, their lives changed a bit.

An intruder began visiting the park.

Her name was Suzu Torikai.

"Oh my, do you want this?"

When Chako stood up on her hind legs and poked her nose into the woman's chair-walker, Suzu brought out a pack of fried chicken, explaining that she'd stopped by on her way home from the supermarket.

"My doctor told me to go outside and get as much sun as possible, you see. I was planning to sun myself on the bench; I had no idea someone so adorable was already using it." As she spoke, Suzu picked Chako up. The fine, crepe-like wrinkles at the outer corners of her eyes deepened, and she looked very soft and kind.

He almost asked, *Would you adopt this dog?*

For some reason, though, he couldn't say it.

Suzu shortened Chako's already short name even further, calling her "Chi."

She said she'd spent a long, long time caring for her grandparents and parents, and then they'd died one after another. She'd been living alone ever since. She'd carelessly scorched a pot by forgetting to turn off the burner once, so these days she got most of her meals from the supermarket deli.

"I'm sorry it's just my leftovers, but if you'd like…," she'd say apologetically, and then she'd feed Chako fish sausage or bargain ham and treat Kazushi to inari sushi or the day's special box lunch.

She also told them a bit about herself.

She said she was lonely because practically the only person she'd had to talk to had been her neighbor, and now they'd moved into a nursing home. She said she'd started staying home all the time and had ended up with insomnia, so the hospital had prescribed her some sleeping pills, which worked really well.

"If I go awhile without talking to anyone, it feels as if I might forget my own name, you know? Even if I think, 'Wait, who am I?' there's nobody to ask."

Speaking slowly, at a tempo that made Kazushi feel a bit drowsy, she stroked Chako's head.

Why not adopt a dog, then?

It was only a brief remark, but he just couldn't say it. He also couldn't reveal his own situation to this elderly woman, whose lonely life was gradually being eroded by dementia.

He couldn't even admit that he didn't want to give up Chako.

However, one day, when winter was getting close...

"I'm not going to be here anymore, so please take care of her."

Pushing Chako into Suzu's hands, Kazushi ran out of the park.

A little while after that, he managed to land some on-site work that came with dormitory housing. If Chako had been there, he couldn't have taken it. She was on his mind, though, and once, he went to sneak a look at the park.

Suzu was there, sitting on the bench with Chako on her lap. She was petting the dog's back in a leisurely rhythm, talking to her the whole time, as if she were a small child.

They looked happy.

The new year came, and Kazushi was out of work again. Instead of going back to his old haunt, he started sleeping in a children's park close to the train station. The kids were loud during the day, but there was a handicapped bathroom where he could take shelter from the rain or snow. On top of that, no other homeless people had claimed it as their territory.

However...

Late one night, the noise of firecrackers startled him. When he dashed out of the bathroom, someone launched a rocket firework straight at him. The fireball had been targeting his face, but it hit the palm he'd thrown up to protect himself instead, bursting loudly and burning him. If it had hit him in the eye, it would have blinded him.

"The face, aim for the face!"

"Put out his eyes! Get 'im!"

The jeering voices weren't young so much as childish. They belonged to middle schoolers who attended the cram school in front of the station.

He'd blown it. The park hadn't had any other homeless residents because it was a "hunting ground" for middle schoolers trying to vent the stress from their entrance exams.

At the time, though, Kazushi was more angry than afraid.

He was mad enough to kill.

The next thing he knew, he'd grabbed the collar of a kid who hadn't made his escape fast enough, pulled him down, then slammed two or three kicks into him. The boy's groans turned into sobs, and he curled up like a caterpillar. He was shaking, his face a mess of snot and tears.

After one last kick, which he aimed at the kid's face, Kazushi left the park. His shoe felt weird. When he checked the sole, a broken front tooth was stuck in the tread of his sneaker like a pebble.

Oh crud, he thought.

If he'd only bruised the kid's face, he might have skated under the radar, but this level of injury was definitely going to get reported to the police. He probably wouldn't be able to go near that park again.

If they found him, that would be it: They'd dispose of him as summarily as if they'd smashed him with a slipper.

Like a cockroach.

Something whose mere presence was unpleasant. A pest that had to be crushed for the good of the world.

And in that case, why should he be decent to other people? Roaches were only roaches, after all.

Subsequently, all he could say was that the devil got into him.

The next thing he knew, Kazushi was in front of Suzu's house, unlocking her front door. She'd told him she kept a spare key hidden in the flowerpot by the entrance, just in case she accidentally dropped hers.

He was planning to steal some money from her wallet while she was fast asleep. He figured if she woke up, he could tie her up with an electrical cord and threaten her with a knife from the kitchen.

When he stepped in through the front door, he found himself in a living room with an old-fashioned warmth to it. Suzu was there, lying on a futon. She was sleeping like the dead. Only the night-light bulb of the fluorescent lamp was on, and in the dimness, her face could have belonged to an actual corpse.

His heart thumped beneath his ribs. In an impulsive attempt to make sure she was breathing, he reached out toward her face, and then...

...pain shot through the base of his little finger.

It was a dog.

Chako had crawled out from under the comforter, and she crouched low, growling, her muzzle wrinkled. A second later, when he saw beads of blood well up in the outline of a set of teeth, he realized she'd bitten him.

It was as if she'd completely forgotten about Kazushi, who'd lived with her until just a few months ago.

He felt as if she'd told him, *I don't want you.*

The words he'd once heard his mother say came back to him vividly. *Why are you alive?*

For a moment his vision went black, and Chako flew through the air, struck the wall, fell to the floor, and went limp.

At first glance, it looked like she was sleeping, with her tongue out, but she wasn't breathing. Her heart had stopped. Her body was warm, though— it seemed like he might still be able to fix this somehow.

...Until dawn, when he went outside and buried her body under a tree in the garden before Suzu woke up.

After that, it just kept happening.

Suzu would wander through town, looking for the vanished Chako. Kazushi would take the opportunity to creep into her house, borrow the bath, and scavenge for leftovers to keep himself alive.

Before long, Suzu brought home the second "Chi." Kazushi killed that dog, too, but he didn't have the energy to dig a hole in the garden to bury it. He just tossed it into the storage compartment under the kitchen floor and pretended it wasn't there.

Maybe he'd wanted Suzu to notice. However, three dogs, four, five— the number kept growing, and every time, the smell in the house got worse.

He couldn't think about what had happened before, or what might happen later. He couldn't think, period.

He just didn't know anymore. He had no idea how he should live. One phrase kept going around and around in his mind:

Why are you alive?

And now...

...Kazushi was running desperately down a rainy residential street.

No matter how far he ran, he couldn't relax. It felt as if he were in a nightmare with no exit.

He knew why: He was being pursued.

He could hear rough panting. Four-legged footsteps were closing in on him. Even if he turned, he wouldn't see any dogs. But they were right on his heels.

If he stopped, he was done for. Even if he kept running, they'd overtake him eventually.

Spurred on by fear and anxiety, he kept sprinting blindly. He was winded, and his harsh, noisy breathing sounded like a set of bellows.

Then...

"Huh?"

...out of nowhere, a familiar scent cut right in front of him.

It was an animal smell—the stink of a rain-wet dog.

It passed me! Just as he realized this, something solid hit him below the knees.

Before he even had time to gasp, he'd pitched forward. He put his hands out to catch himself; gravel bit into his palms, and he scraped his knees up royally. Just now, something had definitely run into his legs.

"...*Ghk.* Ow..."

When he groaned and tried to get up, he realized he was right under a streetlamp. Pallid, artificial light poured down over a shallow puddle on the pavement.

Splish. A small ring of ripples spread over the surface.

Splash-splash, splash.

It was as if invisible dogs were running through the puddle. He heard a low growl. The footsteps edged closer to him from all sides.

He was surrounded.

"Ee, eeep!"

Kazushi bolted like a rabbit, and then another impact ran through his legs.

He couldn't even put his hands out to catch himself this time, and his face plowed into the asphalt. He hit his forehead so hard, he saw sparks. The fall took off a big patch of skin, and a second later, thick blood welled up, spilling over. His face was practically covered in it.

"S-spare m—!"

From that point on, it was just more of the same.

Every time something rammed into his legs, he'd scrape his cheeks, wrench his ankles, break a tooth, split his lip. He might have broken his nose, too.

Even so, the howls and footsteps of the invisible dogs wouldn't let him stop.

He was being hounded.

They were like hunting dogs, running down their prey.

And then…

…like a surprise attack, a red light darted into view. Beside a sign that said, ROAD CLOSED, there was a glowing red light with the word *Construction* on it. They were relocating a water supply line.

Beyond several construction cones set close together in a huddle, there was a tapering pit about two meters deep.

No.

Kazushi gulped audibly, swallowing saliva that tasted like blood.

He'd figured it out: The invisible dogs had intentionally driven him here. They were planning to drop him into that hole.

I've got to run.

They'll kill me.

Legs trembling, he tried to turn back, but then…

"...Huh?"

...a *thud* to end all thuds ran through his chest. It was as if all the dogs had launched themselves off the road and body-slammed him at once.

The next moment, the soles of his sneakers were airborne. The world seemed to flip, and a brief floating sensation swept over him. Before Kazushi could process what that meant, the impact sent him flying backward over the cones, and then he was falling headfirst.

When he came to, he was at the bottom of the pit, looking up at a round patch of sky. For a moment, the light of the warning lamp seemed to turn the radiating streaks of rain into red lines.

He couldn't sense the dogs anywhere now. It could have been all in his head, a one-man play fueled by delusions and hallucinations.

The hunt was over.

He tried to squirm, but he couldn't move. The back of his head hurt. Invisible hands seemed to be hammering a red-hot stake into it. It felt as if his skull was cracking—actually, he probably *had* cracked it.

The split in his head pulsed, throbbing. It felt like there was a heart embedded in the back of his skull. The blood that spilled out with every beat was rapidly weakening the heart in his chest.

I have to yell for help, he thought, but all that came out of his throat was a damp groan. He couldn't even raise his voice, and his vision was gradually dimming.

The area was hushed and still, and he couldn't hear any passing footsteps or cars. This road hadn't had much traffic to begin with, and now there was a ROAD CLOSED sign urging passersby to detour.

It was entirely possible that no one would notice him until construction resumed the next morning and they found his corpse at the bottom of the hole.

Oh, I see... I'm gonna die here.

Once he'd realized that, everything suddenly seemed like too much work. Running around trying to escape had only earned him more pain, and it seemed completely ridiculous. He didn't want to hurt or suffer or struggle, but he hadn't lived seriously enough to cling to life.

If I die here, it will all be over, he thought, exhaling with something a lot like relief. Just then, he heard damp, panting breath, followed by the sound of small feet on gravel.

It was here. Very, very close to him.

The dog was probably by itself. Its footsteps sounded a little unsteady, but it was coming straight toward him.

Kazushi could move his eyes a little, but the red light on the street didn't reach the depths of the pit, and his surroundings were pitch black. He couldn't see a thing.

Then something touched the fingers of his upturned hand.

A flood of nostalgia told him what the sensation was: a moist nose, pressed against his fingertips.

It's Chako.

He just assumed she was going to bite him. She'd chew his fingers off as payback because he'd kicked her to death. After what he'd done, he couldn't hope for anything better.

But then a hot tongue licked the base of his little finger.

That triggered a memory.

Before she'd licked his face or hand, Chako had always sniffed him. It was as if she was checking to make sure the person in front of her was actually Kazushi.

Abruptly, a possibility occurred to him.

Could it be…?

Several remembered fragments clicked into place like puzzle pieces.

Had Chako's eyes been weak?

Maybe she'd always sniffed Kazushi before wagging her tail or licking him because, if she hadn't, she genuinely wouldn't have known it was him.

Come to think of it, if she couldn't see the ground very well, that would explain her slightly awkward gait and the way she pestered him to pick her up for steps, even tiny ones. That might have been why her previous owner had abandoned her, too.

Then wait, don't tell me… Back then…

When Chako bit Kazushi after they'd been separated for several months, had it been because she thought he was just an intruder who'd appeared out of nowhere? With her bad eyes, she hadn't realized it was him. If she'd only bared her fangs at him in a desperate attempt to protect Suzu...

"No..." His dazed murmur was cut off by a bloody cough.

Chako was still licking the base of his little finger. She whined softly, as if she was worried.

And then, finally, it hit Kazushi.

That was where she'd bitten him.

No, it can't be...

If the Chako here with him now was a ghost...

What if, in the moment before she died, she'd realized that the intruder she'd bitten was Kazushi?

What if the emotion that had stayed with her to the very end wasn't anger or resentment but guilt about the fact that she'd bitten him?

What if she'd been worried that she'd hurt him, harmed him, and she'd wanted to lick his wound and get his forgiveness so they could be friends again...?

Don't tell me, even after she died, all this time...

Had she wanted to apologize to him? So that she'd be able to play and sleep and walk beside him again? So that they could be together, man and dog?

The scream that tried to tear its way out of Kazushi's throat vanished into a blood-choked cough, and all that was left was a wordless groan.

It almost sounded like the cry of an animal.

✳

The farther Seiji ran, the harder it poured.

He ran this way and that down narrow alleys, searching for the dogs that had turned into *sunekosuri* and the guy they were chasing. From overhead, he would have looked like a rat in a maze.

He managed to run at full speed only at the beginning, then he promptly got winded. His vision rocked with every step he took. His strength was so tapped out that his knees had gone watery.

He ran and ran, but the next thing he knew, he was basically just walking. Somewhere in there, his breath had turned white. There was sleet mingled with the rain, and he felt like he might freeze to death on his feet.

He started to suspect it might all be pointless. It had been presumptuous of him to try to affect somebody else's life in the first place.

He couldn't do a thing, but there was no need to. Trying to save someone was out of the question. That was how he'd lived all this time.

"But...," Seiji muttered. He shook his head like a dog, clearing off the rain. *Shiroshi would stop them for sure.*

The moment he thought that, Odoro's sharp remark echoed in his ears.

"You two are most definitely the heretics here."

He was probably right. Still, Shiroshi wasn't wrong, either. Odoro weighed the gravity of the crime, then handed down a suitable punishment. In contrast, Shiroshi tried to understand the person who'd committed the crime.

The sinner and the one sinned against.

Both were human. Hopelessly human, as far as Shiroshi was concerned.

They were wounded, deceived, and harmed.

They also inflicted wounds, deceived others, and did harm.

As victims, they prayed that criminals would be punished.

As criminals, they hoped for a chance to atone.

That was how humans were.

What if someone killed me?

What if I killed someone else?

Whichever way that balance tilted, *that* was the judgment Shiroshi handed down.

In that moment, something occurred to Seiji. He almost wished it hadn't.

You know, I'm not actually sure Shiroshi is cut out to be the Demon King.

Come to think of it... No, he didn't even need to think about it.

Shiroshi knew people too well.

Even if he managed to win the throne...wouldn't the only thing waiting for him there be unimaginable loneliness? He'd be the only one with a human heart, surrounded by supernatural attendants.

All alone.

Maybe that was why Shiroshi was so half-hearted about judging sinners: because he didn't want to live like that.

Even if it was the one and only way to win his freedom.

Does that mean Shiroshi doesn't know how he should live, either?

Abruptly, Seiji heard a siren. A streak of red lanced across his vision, and then a red-and-white vehicle turned the corner.

An ambulance.

A chill ran down Seiji's spine, and his blood froze. His legs threatened to start shaking, but he kept them under control and walked around the corner, a little unsteadily.

The siren had already been turned off, but its red light was still flashing. A crowd of rubberneckers with umbrellas had gathered around the ambulance.

Someone on a stretcher was being loaded into the back.

An arm hung limply over the side, so incredibly pale that the sight burned itself onto Seiji's retinas. It could have belonged to a bloodless corpse.

No, don't tell me…

Staggering, Seiji went closer. Then he noticed a big pit in the road up ahead—a construction site.

He also saw the puddle of blood at the bottom of the pit and a sneaker with a hole in its heel. It had probably fallen off when they were lifting the guy out.

Oh, I see. So he died.

The air seemed too thin, and the strength went out of Seiji's legs. He felt as if he might tumble into that hole, and his feet clung to the pavement as if they'd grown roots. He couldn't move.

A sense of futility washed over him, and Seiji found himself repeating one phrase, over and over.

I was too late.

I was too late again.

✳

Two hours later, at the Rindou Detective Agency…

Seiji had come back as wet as a drowned rat. When he gave an enormous, flamboyant sneeze, Odoro frowned in disgust and threw a bath towel at him.

Snuffling, Seiji rubbed down his soaked head and body, then huddled up with the towel pulled over his head and around his shoulders like a cloak. At that point, finally, he started to feel like himself again.

He didn't have the strength to move a finger anymore, but his teeth wouldn't stop chattering. Intense chills raced through him, and his head ached as though he'd been punched in the temple. He was coming down with a cold.

Still, he'd been running around in the freezing rain without an umbrella, so maybe he was lucky to have gotten off this lightly.

After all, the other guy who'd been out wandering in the rain had died from a fall into a construction site. Not only that, but he'd been driven there by *sunekosuri*, the ghosts of the dogs he'd killed.

You reap what you sow. Ill begets ill. What goes around comes around. His death probably matched those sayings pretty well… At least as far as the *oni* who'd handed out Hell's punishment was concerned.

"Dammit!" Seiji muttered to himself, and it set off a coughing fit he couldn't stop.

Between the fatigue and the headache, his mind was hazy. On the other hand, he felt the urge to start yelling at the top of his lungs. Cussing somebody out now wouldn't help anything, though.

That guy was dead. He wouldn't come back.

That was a fact, and nothing could change it.

Son of a bitch, Seiji swore silently, rolling onto his side on the floor.

That was when the chair beside the window caught his eye. That leather upholstered armchair, the one somebody had once treasured. It had probably been Ibara Rindou's regular seat.

…*Hm?*

Just then, an unpleasant chill ran down Seiji's spine.

Something was off here. He was sure of it.

He couldn't put his finger on what, though.

He felt an overwhelming sense of unease, and his heart began to race. A strange premonition came over him that he couldn't afford to stay in this place. Then it gelled into near certainty, and the hair on the back of his neck stood on end.

There was tension, anxiety, and fear.

And at the same time, he had an odd feeling of déjà vu. It was almost... Yes, almost like what he'd felt just before the wildfire that night, when he'd left the deserted temple by himself.

It felt like he was being watched.

As if a snake's unblinking eyes were fixed on him, drinking him in.

"U-um... I think there's something weird about that chair," Seiji started to say, although even he didn't know exactly what he was trying to get across. He pointed at the armchair. "Uh, if you look closely, there's this spot on its back that came apart, then was messily sewn up with thread in the same color. It's just, it really doesn't seem like the sort of thing you'd do."

Seiji tried to put himself in Odoro's shoes and imagine it.

If Shiroshi never came back, and his chair became like a memento... If the seat fabric tore, could Seiji bring himself to use his shaky sewing skills to clumsily patch it up on his own?

No way.

He'd either leave it as it was, or he'd have it repaired professionally. On top of that, as a rule, Odoro seemed to completely avoid looking at the chair. Even if his life were on the line, he'd never be able to do it.

However—no, for that very reason—the situation raised a question. After all, Odoro was the only one at the agency now.

"So *who mended that?*"

Odoro had been listening dubiously, but at this question, a tremendous surge of agitation swept over his face. Grabbing a letter opener from the desk, he ran to the chair by the window and sliced through the mended bit. An object emerged from behind it: a small black box. It looked like the sort of compact listening device that showed up in movies.

"When on earth…?" Odoro muttered, dazed.

Then, out of nowhere, they heard a soft *creak*. One of the sections of the document shelf at the back of the study had swung open, almost like a hidden door—no, that was *exactly* what it was.

"Huh?"

A young man Seiji didn't recognize stepped through it.

Even in the gloom, his white shoulder-length hair had a beautiful luster. Behind his long bangs, his eyes were a terribly familiar amber.

In his dark Inverness cape, his thin frame looked more like a magician's than like a detective's. Maybe it was because, even though he was fairly tall, there was something rather feminine about him.

He was thin, delicate, and soft.

…And yet he possessed the intimidating, spine-chilling beauty of a predator. On top of that, he was holding a sinister-looking shotgun.

Odoro's eyes were so wide that his eyelids seemed liable to tear at the corners, and he'd gone as still as a statue. Finally, his trembling lips moved slightly.

"Ibara."

It was as if he were calling someone who'd returned from the abyss. His twin, who was supposed to be dead.

As if in response, the gun in the ghost's hands came up. Removing an earpiece that seemed to be connected to the listening device they'd found, he said:

"You're in the way."

There was a roar.

A sickeningly vivid red mist bloomed like a flower. The man's pale finger had pulled the trigger as smoothly as the falling blade of a guillotine.

For a few seconds, silence fell.

Then Odoro staggered backward and collapsed to the floor. He'd been shot through the left shoulder; it was drenched with dark blood. The gun hadn't been loaded with buckshot, so he'd been hit in only one place, but the bleeding showed no sign of slowing down. Of course not: The wound was far too big. It was practically a crater.

Looking down at him arrogantly, Ibara wiped a streak of his victim's blood off his cheek. "You know I've never been good at sewing. That was the only place where I could be sure you'd never find it, though. That chair was a memento of me, after all. I assumed a sentimentalist like you wouldn't even be able to take a proper look at it."

His voice was nearly a whisper. He spoke without inflection, almost as if he were reading a poem aloud.

He gazed at Odoro through half-open eyes, as if he found this tiresome. "You may be my little brother, but that was pathetic. Still, it was very like you." Slowly bending down, he grabbed a handful of hair at the back of Odoro's head and pulled, bringing his face closer. "You haven't changed. You show no mercy to the strong, but you can't ignore small children or the elderly—and you have a particular soft spot for animals. That's why I found that client for you. I knew you were sure to act, even if it meant ignoring the Enma Ministry's orders. I had some business outside that I wanted to take care of today, you see."

Then Suzu had gotten that business card either from Ibara himself or from an accomplice. Not only that, but it had been Ibara who'd suggested that she visit the agency today.

No, but…wasn't he dead? Seiji thought, desperately confused.

Odoro gave a wet, murky cough. He was spitting up blood. Wheezing should have been all he could manage. Even so, his pale lips moved; for a moment, it looked as if he'd even forgotten the pain he was in.

"…Ibara?"

His twin's smile deepened as far as it would go.

"If possible, I never wanted to hear you say my name again."

Straightening up, he brought his shoe down, stomping on his brother's bloody wound. Bone snapped and crunched, and Odoro roared. It sounded like the howl of a dying animal.

As Ibara looked at his brother, who'd finally blacked out, there was something like pity in his eyes. Then, with a clank, he slid the forestock back.

He'd ejected the spent shell…and loaded a fresh one.

"N-no, wait! Please wait!" Seiji said impulsively. Dashing over to Odoro, he searched inside his suit jacket, found a handkerchief, and pressed it to the wound on his shoulder. It wouldn't come close to stopping the bleeding, but it was still better than nothing.

…Technically, he didn't care if this guy died.

Even so…

He treasured that chair his brother left behind, and now this?

Being shot dead by somebody he cared about that much would be utterly… No. It was just too cruel.

"I see. You really are an impressively stupid dog," Ibara said, abruptly narrowing his eyes. Shifting his shotgun to his left hand, he raised his right, as casually as if he meant to swat a fly.

"Out of the way."

His hand began to descend, headed straight for the side of Seiji's face, and then…

"Huh?"

…something flew toward them and struck Ibara's fingers. When Seiji took a closer look, it turned out to be a very familiar black leather ankle boot.

Déjà vu.

Hadn't he been through something extremely similar just three months ago? The two sets of footsteps he heard from the spiral staircase on the left only strengthened the resemblance.

"Well, this is even uglier than I'd anticipated."

So did that voice, as dignified as a white peony in bloom.

"It's been a long time, Ibara. You as well, Seiji."

The next thing Seiji knew, he was looking at a small white back.

It was right there, half a step in front of him, as if to shield him.

It's Shiroshi.

"Wh-why…?" he tried to ask, but his voice came out sounding delirious.

Turning back quickly, Shiroshi put an index finger to his lips. *Does he want me to be quiet? Or maybe he means "Leave this to me."*

Meanwhile, Beniko was performing first aid on Odoro's bloodied body.

...For some reason, as soon as Seiji began to think that the man might survive, he abruptly stopped caring.

Ibara had tipped the gun back so that its barrel lay across his shoulder. He cocked his head, birdlike. "It's been, what, three days?"

"Yes, it seemed all the players were finally in place, so I took the liberty of coming back to life."

It was a strange sight.

Black.

White.

As the pair faced each other from a distance, they seemed like complete opposites, yet also terribly similar. It was as if they were mirror images of each other.

Shiroshi tilted his head in the other direction. "You aren't going to say 'But you're supposed to be dead,' then?"

"As the villain, I probably should, shouldn't I? I did have the feeling you weren't, though. Frankly, the one Kazutora killed was far too easy."

"I see. And that's why you hid yourself so carefully?"

What's he talking about? Seiji was perplexed.

"Let me relate what happened *after you killed me.* In fact, I came back safely three days ago, on the day of the wildfire. Your misdeeds were exposed as soon as you let me slip through your fingers. For the past three days, I've been working with the Enma Ministry to locate you. We kept me officially missing, disguising the search for you as a search for me."

What?

"Takamura informed you that Great King Enma had personally taken command of the search for the mastermind, didn't he, Seiji? That separate unit was actually the main force. In other words, this wasn't a search for a criminal but a fox hunt."

So it hadn't been Shiroshi or Seiji who was being hunted but Ibara, who should technically have been the hunter.

However...

"No matter how we searched, we couldn't trace your movements. Then today, I had a sudden thought. Although I'd rather we weren't, if you and

I were similar, I thought we might have chosen similar places to go to ground. 'It's always darkest under the lighthouse,' as the saying goes. It was possible you'd returned to the place you knew best."

Ah. That had been the Rindou Detective Agency, then.

"Therefore."

"Huh?"

Abruptly, Shiroshi did something unexpected.

Sticking a hand into Seiji's coat pocket, he pulled out his pack of cigarettes. It was the one where he'd found the twisted paper note. When Shiroshi turned it upside down and tapped on the base, a small object rolled out onto his palm: a listening device even more compact than the one in the chair.

"Oh," Seiji said, startled.

"Please visit Odoro's detective agency and stay there for as long as you can."

Shiroshi had given him those instructions through Beniko so that he would go to the place he suspected Ibara was hiding, as his "ears."

Oh, yeah. I completely forgot.

That's right—scheming was what Shiroshi did best.

"As they say, 'A snake half-killed will return to bite you.' If you put someone through something awful, then fail to finish them off, they'll retaliate later—which is exactly what's happening to you now."

The protagonist of this dramatic reversal smiled like a white peony in full bloom. "Do you remember what I said earlier? 'On principle, I only fight opponents I know I can defeat.' Naturally, that includes you, Ibara." He tilted his head in a way that made him seem very young. "I apologize if I've offended you. I'm merely being myself," he said, his face clearly that of a victor.

"…Oh yes?" Ibara murmured. His voice was flat, and the air went tense.

His finger connected with the trigger, and by the time Seiji gasped, the muzzle had snapped up to point at Shiroshi. It was too close, too fast—there was no time to run.

A shot rang out.

With a dry noise, the bullet gouged the floor…at *Ibara Rindou's* feet. His eyes widened in surprise.

A moment before his shotgun could fire, a shot from directly in front of him had scarred the floor at his feet.

"Um, I borrowed this from Odoro when I got the handkerchief out of his jacket," said Seiji.

Stepping in front of Shiroshi—who looked uncharacteristically startled—he'd leveled the revolver Odoro had been carrying for self-defense and fired at Ibara. Still threatening him with the gun, Seiji glared at him. "The next one won't be a warning."

In order to fire, he'd had to muster all the fuzzy knowledge he'd picked up from reading magazines in the aisles at convenience stores. But the bullet had struck the floor accurately, right at Ibara's feet.

To a bystander, it would probably have looked like a warning shot, fired as a restraint.

Yes, that was how it had *looked*.

"What were you actually trying to hit?" Shiroshi whispered.

His head, Seiji mouthed silently.

"…I see. Next time, let me do it."

That would be great!

On the inside, the pressure of taking a second shot had Seiji nearly in tears. But as he was secretly feeling relieved…

"Heh-heh-heh."

…Ibara had begun to chuckle. He sounded amused, entertained. From the look in his eyes, he could have been watching a dog perform a trick with his master.

"I see. You truly are a stupid dog. Still, I suppose that means you and your master suit each other well." Ibara glanced at Odoro, then turned and started toward the spiral staircase, as if he'd lost interest.

"What are you really trying to accomplish?" Shiroshi called after him.

The white-haired revenant looked back over his shoulder with a smile that was almost alluring.

"That should have been obvious from the start."

That was all he said, and then he vanished like a ghost on a dark night. Only a hush was left, like the stillness after the wind has died. Beniko had finished performing first aid on Odoro, and a faint trace of color seemed to be returning to him.

All else aside, it was over.

"Um, Shiro…" Seiji tried to call the boy's name, but his throat closed up on him. His chest grew tight, and his trachea spasmed. Still, when he moved his lips desperately, the word came out, carrying what felt like years of nostalgia. "…Shiroshi."

"Yes?"

"Are you really you?"

"Yes."

Seiji was relieved—too relieved; the strength went out of his legs, and he sat down right there on the floor.

"My, my." Smiling wryly, Shiroshi ruffled his hair. Seiji felt the depths of his eyes and nose sting, and he softly bit his lip.

Still, at this point, the mere fact that Shiroshi's hand was there made Seiji feel as if he could put up with anything.

Shiroshi's alive.

He was right here next to him.

"Now then, we should be going… Can you stand?" Shiroshi held out a hand, and Seiji took it. The hand was as pale as bone or wax, but there was a living, human warmth to it.

Even if it didn't belong to a human like he was.

"Let's go home, shall we, Seiji?"

"Yes!"

Seiji set off after Shiroshi's small back.

He stayed half a step behind, just like always.

✳

"Let me ask you one final thing. What is it that you wish to do right now?"

He felt as if he'd heard someone ask that question, right before he passed out. The asker had been a boy, black-haired and dressed in what looked like a burial robe.

So this is Death, huh? That made sense to Kazushi, and he answered the boy.

Even if it turned out he was just talking to himself for the last time, he didn't care.

The next time he opened his eyes, he was in bed in a hospital room.

Why am I alive? he thought. But according to the doctor and nurses, he'd genuinely sustained serious injuries. They told him that if he'd been reported even a minute later, he would have died.

The caller had sounded like a boy, but they still didn't know who it was.

Apparently, his bandaged, gauze-covered face would never be the same. They weren't sure if hair would ever grow over the wounded spot on the back of his head, either.

Two weeks after Kazushi was admitted, he slipped out of the ward, then headed straight for the police station. It wasn't as if he had any way to pay his hospital bill.

He'd broken the tooth of a middle schooler who'd been hunting homeless people.

He'd illegally entered Suzu's house countless times, and he'd killed five dogs.

He didn't know how much of a sentence any of those things would carry. They were crimes, though. That much was undeniable.

And then…

…Kazushi found himself standing in that park.

Bright autumn sunlight streamed down over the bench, and fallen leaves covered the ground in a dappled carpet. When he drew a breath, he thought it smelled like light.

The figure he'd been searching for was there. Suzu was sitting on the bench, nodding drowsily, that chair-walker with the flower-patterned bag at her side.

Kazushi felt the depths of his throat begin to quiver. He realized he was biting his lip.

Even he didn't know why he'd come here, after all this time.

But…

He went closer to the bench, dead leaves crackling under his feet. Suzu looked up. She blinked slowly, like a cat dozing in the sun.

Their eyes met.

I have to say something, he thought, but all his lips would do was tremble. His throat had gone dry, and he couldn't make a sound. His heart was jumping around as if he'd developed an arrhythmia, and he felt his underarms grow damp with sweat.

"It's a lovely day, isn't it?" Suzu said. The sun wasn't all that bright, but she narrowed her eyes, as if it dazzled her.

She doesn't recognize me, he thought.

She hadn't registered who was standing in front of her. Her eyes were only vaguely turned in his direction; she might not even have realized there was a person there at all.

Or so he thought, but…

"Huh?"

Abruptly, Suzu knelt formally on the bench and bowed very, very deeply to him. She scuffed her forehead on the peeling paint, again and again. Her hands trembled, the wrinkles on them even deeper than they'd been in the gloom under that night-light.

"I'm sorry. I'm so sorry. I've lost Chi. Even though she was so important to you. Even though I was happy that you'd counted on me, and that I could help you. I'm so sorry." *I'm sorry*, she repeated over and over.

"…Oh."

Kazushi tried to speak, but the words still wouldn't come.

It couldn't be—had Suzu searched for Chi so desperately because she'd been taking care of her for him?

Someone had finally been kind enough to count on her, she said. She'd finally been able to help someone.

Kazushi knew better than anyone how much it hurt when nobody needed you, how lonely and futile your life felt. If Suzu was like him…

Chi had suddenly vanished, and Suzu had gone around looking and looking for her.

She'd been silently apologizing to Kazushi the whole time.

If that was what had worn her down like this…

Don't tell me…

When she'd finally started to see stray dogs that looked nothing like Chi as Chi… When her dementia had gotten bad enough to make that possible…

Had all of it been Kazushi's fault?

In that moment, he felt something inside him break.

His eyes blurred. The strength went out of his knees, and he crumpled to the ground. Watery snot ran down the back of his throat, and he choked again and again. Even then, it took him a while to realize he was crying.

"I…ry!" he shrieked, shoulders shaking, sobbing like a child. He pressed his forehead to the ground, saying the words over and over with an intensity that nearly split his throat.

Kazushi had finally remembered. When the boy in the white kimono had asked him, "What is it that you wish to do right now?" he'd simply said, "I want to apologize."

Even though apologizing wouldn't help anything. Even though he knew he'd never be forgiven, that everything was broken past saving.

Even so, the truth was that he'd always, always wanted to say he was sorry.

Ever since he'd stood frozen in the entryway at his childhood home, dressed in his uniform, gripping his schoolbag with a sweaty palm.

I'm sorry I can't do it right.

I'm sorry I can't live properly.

I'm sorry I'm like this.

I made you unhappy. I hit you.

I made you die. I killed you.

"…I'm……ry."

Kazushi repeated himself until his throat was hoarse. At some point, he realized Suzu had crouched down beside him.

Her warm hand was stroking his back. That painfully thin, wrinkled hand stroked him slowly, over and over, just as she'd once petted Chako.

As if she were caring for something weak and precious.

There was no longer anything he could say but *I'm sorry.* Even if those words had no meaning anymore.

Even so, the hand on his back was warm.

For now...I'm still alive.

MYSTERY 3

FILICIDE, OR EPILOGUE

The time after a storm is very quiet.

As soon as he and Shiroshi got back to the house, Seiji passed out and slept like a log. When he woke up, life had returned to normal. That is to say, he, Beniko, and Shiroshi were all there together.

It was midnight. Outside, it sounded as if it was still raining. When Seiji sat up in bed—which took some doing—Shiroshi was sitting in a chair by his bedside, reading.

"You're awake." He smiled.

Seiji had seen this before. Right now, the fact that he was getting to see it again made him happier than anything.

"Um, welcome ho— *Dwachoo!*"

"My, my." Smiling wryly, Shiroshi picked up a thermos from the bedside table. "Here you are. Really, it seems as if all it takes to put humans at death's door is a moment's inattention." Speaking as if he felt the words keenly, Shiroshi filled a mug with the contents of the thermos and offered it to Seiji. This was nothing new, but he was talking like a grade school kid who'd forgotten to water the morning glories.

Shooting him a look from under half-lowered eyelids, Seiji drank his hot ginger-water with honey. Soon, as if the liquid had reminded it, his stomach started clamoring that it was empty, so they asked Beniko for some of the rice porridge she'd made for the following day's breakfast.

The grime that had built up over the past three days had apparently bothered Beniko, so she planned to stay up all night to do a deep housecleaning. She couldn't have been more herself if she'd tried.

Between this and that, Seiji practically worshipped Beniko when she appeared with the tray. He'd scooped up a spoonful of porridge topped with steamed chicken and chopped leek and was chewing, when… "Huh?! So that guy survived?"

"Yes, I called an ambulance. I believe he'll live."

They were talking about the young man who'd been chased into the pit at the construction site by *sunekosuri*. Seiji had just assumed he'd died, but Shiroshi had actually saved him.

Seiji thought that was a good thing, although he wasn't positive he'd still be able to see it that way later.

"Does that mean you heard me and Odoro talking through those bugged cigarettes?"

"Yes, that's right."

"You must have been pretty close, then. Actually, where were you?" In spite of himself, Seiji sounded resentful. Really, though, after Shiroshi had gone three full days without making contact, he thought he could probably punch him once and still be owed a significant amount in damages.

"Heh-heh-heh. Right beside you, Seiji."

Hm? Where would that have been?

"Here, in this house. I assumed Beniko's identity three days ago."

Wha—? Oh come on, no way, that's ridiculous!

"Since we have the opportunity, I'll explain from the beginning. By custom, those who inherit the blood of Sanmoto Gorouzaemon are given a name associated with a color. My own name indicates a pure white, unsullied state. My older brother Hibana's name includes the character for 'scarlet.' And there is one that includes 'crimson'—Beniko's."

Seiji made an involuntary, startled noise.

Come to think of it, that was true. Seiji's own name had "blue" in it, and he was just their freeloader, so he'd never given it much thought.

"Huh? Then Beniko is really your—" He'd meant to say *sister*, but Shiroshi shook his head.

"No, Beniko was originally a goldfish. However, my father gave her his blood and transformed her into a yokai."

Apparently, she could now assume both human and goldfish forms. Who'd have believed she was actually an ex-goldfish?

"Now then, proof trumps argument. First, take a look at this photograph."

Shiroshi held out what looked like a perfectly normal photo of the two of them. Shiroshi was sitting with a large book lying open near his hand, while Beniko stood beside him, holding a tray.

… They both look pretty much the way they do now.

"All right, now use this fountain pen to black out my eyes."

"Um, like this? …Wha—? Aaaaaah!"

Now there were two Benikos.

No, that wasn't it. The moment he'd colored in the whites of Shiroshi's eyes, the boy had become Beniko.

Those black eyes of hers made such a strong impression that Seiji had never noticed, but their facial features were practically identical. It wasn't just a vague family resemblance. They could have been twins.

"C-come to think of it, didn't you say you were about the same height?"

Shiroshi had said their heights were the same if Beniko took off her high-heeled boots. In other words, they were identical there, too.

"You see, Beniko was intentionally made that way. As a matter of fact, she had an older twin brother. His name was Shion, and he was my body double. You remember the goldfish in the bay window in the hall, don't you? That was Shion."

He did. That goldfish bowl had been there ever since Seiji first came to the house, and the goldfish in it had looked a lot like Beniko. So that had been her big brother?

"As a rule, he stayed here. Because of that incident in Nagasaki, however, I had Shion accompany us on our recent excursion."

"Huh? How?"

"I carried him in a small glass jar in my Shingen bag. I kept both Shion and a small bottle of strong acid for self-defense with me at all times."

That's right. Seiji remembered seeing *two* bottles in the bottom of the Shingen bag in the train on the way to the inn. He'd assumed Shiroshi had bought something to drink, but…

"B-but the goldfish bowl looked the same as always when we left. From what you're saying, shouldn't it have been emp—?"

Before Seiji finished his question, a possibility occurred to him.

When he'd gotten back to the house, the goldfish had somehow changed from male to female. In other words…

"Yes, that was Beniko. I had her return to her fish form and take Shion's place in the goldfish bowl."

That night, the one who'd been at Shiroshi's side had been Shion, not Beniko.

After Seiji went down the mountain alone, when Shiroshi had stayed behind in the deserted temple with the false Mayuka, Ibara's plot had put him in mortal danger.

Shiroshi had bought time by using the acid on Kazutora, his pursuer. At that point, he'd switched places with Shion, who'd taken a human form identical to his.

Then, as his substitute, Shion had…

"He died," said Beniko. "That was my brother's duty."

"…I've caused your family suffering," said Shiroshi.

"No, it's an honor." Beniko set a hand on Shiroshi's shoulder, as if to console him, and he gently covered it with his own. With their shared history, even that small gesture was enough.

However…

"To be honest, my brother spent most of his life as a fish, so he still had the emotions of a fish and the intelligence of a fish… Really, he was just a fish."

That's not very appropriate! Seiji, teary-eyed, came pretty close to yelling as much, but he figured Beniko had spoken out of consideration for Shiroshi. Her master was kind, and she wanted him to worry as little as possible.

"Then I changed into some of Beniko's clothes, put in black color contacts, and rejoined you, Seiji."

So the Beniko who'd darted out of the flames had actually been Shiroshi.

"B-but then, why were you crying…?"

He was thinking of the single tear that had trickled from those black, black eyes.

"Master Shiroshi is dead."

That tear was what had made him believe in Shiroshi's death, and yet…

"Ah. Embarrassingly, the contacts didn't agree with me."

"…Excuse me, Beniko? Can I hit him, just once?"

"You may do as you please."

Seiji's eyes were steadier than they'd ever been, but just as he accepted the tray from Beniko…

"Oh, that's the Enma Ministry." Clearing his throat in a way that sounded patently forced, Shiroshi grabbed his smartphone and hustled out into the hall to take the exquisitely timed call. *Dammit, he's really quick at running.*

Before long, he came back. "Well, if the results of the Enma Ministry's private inquiry are to be believed, it's now certain that the mastermind was Shinno Akugorou. They say it's likely that he took advantage of the killings during the battle over the succession to make it appear as if Ibara, his actual heir, had died, and install his younger brother Odoro in his place. Then Ibara began working covertly, doing Akugorou's bidding. It's even possible that having the thirteen brothers kill each other was a distraction intended to set the stage for this situation."

"…That's completely horrible."

In other words, it was very likely that Odoro and his brothers had been ordered to kill each other simply to lay the foundation for this conspiracy.

Could a father really do something like that to his own children?

In addition, Odoro had apparently known nothing of his father's scheme.

He'd simply grieved the death of his twin and attempted to shoulder the weight of his twelve brothers' lives while carrying out his duties as heir.

It was just too brutal.

And then…

Beniko's head abruptly came up and swiveled to one side. "Excuse me. It seems we have a guest."

"My, at this hour?"

"I believe it's one of your father's messengers," she said, and she went out to meet them.

"Um, now that you mention it, did your father say anything about this…?" Seiji trailed off midsentence. From Shiroshi's profile, he seemed to be deep in thought.

"I really can't believe that was Ibara's only objective," he murmured quietly. The words felt like the first drop from a rain cloud. "I've been thinking, all this time—wondering if he truly is like me. It's possible that the one he resembles isn't me, but…"

They heard footsteps. It took Seiji a full fifteen seconds to realize they belonged to Beniko. After all, *they were flustered*. Impossibly so for Beniko, who was always calm and collected.

On top of that…

"Master Shiroshi."

…when Beniko flung open the door, her face was obviously pale.

"Your father—Demon King Sanmoto Gorouzaemon *has passed away*. In addition, it appears that Evil God Shinno Akugorou perished at some point last night."

In that moment, a whisper seemed to rise in Seiji's mind.

The voice was Ibara Rindou's.

"I had some business outside that I wanted to take care of today."

Come to think of it, after Seiji and Odoro had departed for Suzu's house and Ibara had left his hiding place at the Rindou Detective Agency…where had he gone, and what had he done?

"…Oh, I see. I finally understand," Shiroshi murmured. He'd gone as pale as a corpse as well. His voice was trembling slightly, as if he'd just looked into the depths of Hell.

At last, Seiji thought he knew what Ibara really meant when he answered Shiroshi's question about his true intentions.

Patricide.

In this world, there may be a child who devours his own parent.

The End

MAJOR WORKS REFERENCED

Akasaka, Norio, ed. *The Gallery Known as "Story."* Shinyosha, 1992.

Ashida, Seijirou. *The Dictionary of Animal Worship.* Hokushindo, 1999.

Chiba, Mikio. *The Comprehensive Encyclopedia of Yokai and Monsters.* Kodansha, 1991.

Fukui, Eiichi. *Snakes and Women and Bells.* Gihodo Shuppan, 2012.

Iijima, Yuko (of the Big Issue Japan Foundation). *Report: Homeless Youth.* Chikuma Shobo, 2011.

Kamon, Nanami. *The Hall of Mystic Animals.* Shueisha, 2014.

Kwai, Vol. 0018. Kadokawa Shoten, 2005.

Kyogoku, Natsuhiko, text, and Katsumi, Tada ed. *The Yokai Picture Scroll.* Kokushokankokai, 2004.

Miyamoto, Sachie, ed. *The Japanese Yokai File.* Gakken Publishing, 2013.

Miyata, Noboru. *Folklore of Yokai.* Iwanami Shoten, 1985.

Mizuki, Shigeru. *The Big Dictionary of Japanese Yokai.* Compiled by Kenji Murakami. Kadokawa Shoten, 2005.

Murakami, Kenji. *The Yokai Dictionary.* Mainichi Shimbunsha, 2000.

Ooi, Gen. *What Are Elderly Dementia Patients Seeing?* Shinchosha, 2008.

Quarterly Kwai, Issue 1. Kadokawa Shoten, 1998.

Sasama, Yoshihiko. *Snake Tales: Their Mystery and Legend.* Daiichi Shobo, 1991.

Sasama, Yoshihiko. *The Japanese Cryptid Dictionary, Illustrated.* Kashiwa Art Publishing, 1994.

Shimura, Kunihiro, ed. *The Dictionary of Japan's Mysterious Yokai, Grotesques and Enchanters.* Bensei Publishing, 2011.

Shintani, Naoki, ed. *Folklore Studies in Everyday Life 1: One Day.* Yoshikawa Koubunkan, 2003.

Society for the Study of Izumi Kyoka, ed. *Essay Collection: Izumi Kyouka.* Yuseido, 1987.

Taboos of the Japanese: Unlucky Words, Unlucky Directions, Superstitions… What did People Fear? Compiled by Naoki Shintani. Seishun Publishing Co., 2003.

Tada, Katsumi. *Deciphering the Demon Horde.* Kodansha, 1999.

Toriyama Sekien—The Demon Horde's Night Parade. Edited by Atsunobu Inada and Naohi Tanaka. Compiled by Takada Mamoru. Kokushokankokai, 1993.

Takada, Mamoru, rev. Inada, Atsunobu; Tanaka, Naohi, eds. *Toriyama Sekien—The Demon Horde's Night Parade.* Kokushokankokai, 1993.

Tsunemitsu, Tohru. *The Folklore of Gestures: The Magical World and the Mind.* Minerva Shobo, 2006.

Tsutsumi, Kunihiko. *Report on* Jatai: *The Discovery of the Snake of Passion and Edo Period Literature. Journal of Kyoto Seika University,* Issue 27, 2004.

Tsutsumi, Kunihiko. *Report on* Jatai: *Supplement. Journal of Kyoto Seika University,* Issue 28, 2005.

Yamaguchi, Michihiro, ed. *Indifferent Care: Aging, Isolation and Poverty in a Society of Single Elderly.* Gendai Shokan, 2012.

HAVE YOU BEEN TURNED ON TO LIGHT NOVELS YET?

86—EIGHTY-SIX, VOL. 1-13

In truth, there is no such thing as a bloodless war. Beyond the fortified walls protecting the eighty-five Republic Sectors lies the "nonexistent" Eighty-Sixth Sector. The young men and women of this forsaken land are branded the Eighty-Six and, stripped of their humanity, pilot "unmanned" weapons into battle...

Manga adaptation available now!

WOLF & PARCHMENT, VOL. 1-10

The young man Col dreams of one day joining the holy clergy and departs on a journey from the bathhouse, Spice and Wolf. Winfiel Kingdom's prince has invited him to help correct the sins of the Church. But as his travels begin, Col discovers in his luggage a young girl with a wolf's ears and tail named Myuri, who stowed away for the ride!

Manga adaptation available now!

SOLO LEVELING, VOL. 1-8

E-rank hunter Jinwoo Sung has no money, no talent, and no prospects to speak of—and apparently, no luck, either! When he enters a hidden double dungeon one fateful day, he's abandoned by his party and left to die at the hands of some of the most horrific monsters he's ever encountered.

Comic adaptation available now!